IN HER NATURE

In Her Nature

Karen X. Tulchinsky

women's
P R E S S

CANADIAN CATALOGUING IN PUBLICATION DATA
Tulchinsky, Karen X.
  In her nature
ISBN 0-88961-210-2
I. Lesbianism — Fiction. II. Title.
PS8589.U53I5 1995   C813.54   C95-931880-1
PR9199.3.T85T5 1995

A shorter version of *A Different Kind of Love* first appeared in *Lovers,* edited by Amber Coverdale Sumrall (The Crossing Press, 1992). *A Working Dyke's Dream* was first published in *Afterglow,* edited by Karen Barber (Alyson Publications, 1993). *Women Who Make My Knees Weak* appeared in *The Femme Mystique* edited by Lesléa Newman (Alyson Publications, 1995). *The Gay Divorcée* was previously published in *Tangled Sheets,* edited by Rosamund Elwin and Karen X. Tulchinsky (Women's Press, 1995). "The Glory of Love" was written by Billy Hill. "That's Amore" was written by Brooks and Warren, copyright Warner Chappel Music Canada.
Copy editor: Noreen Shanahan
Cover photograph: Dianne Whelan
Cover design: Denise Maxwell
Author photo: Susan Stewart

This book was produced by the collective effort of Women's Press. Women's Press gratefully acknowledges the financial support of the Canada Council and the Ontario Arts Council.

Printed and bound in Canada
1 2 3 4 5 1999 1998 1997 1996 1995

Acknowledgements

There are so many people to thank.

Ann Decter for her encouragement, editing and general help pulling the book together. All of the staff and volunteers at Women's Press. Suzanne Perreault — your support, encouragement and editorial assistance have been instrumental to my writing. Lois Fine for inspiring me to get back to writing after a long absence and for help with the ending of *The Gay Divorcée*. James Johnstone for helping me get through this past year (not to mention feeding me great food and wine whether I needed it or not). Terrie Hamazaki for all of the lovely gifts you bring to me. Sheila Wahsquonaikezhik for helping me with re-writes, and reminding me to breathe, drink water and do wheels on everything. Lee Maracle — what you taught me about writing and about myself was an incredible gift. Joan Nestle for having the courage to write about butch-femme reality when it was unpopular to do so, and paving the way for the rest of us. Dionne Brand for giving me just the right advice at the right time. Shawn Feeney, olev hashalom, for being the first person to teach me what it means to live with AIDS.

Lori (Flatbed) Kosciuw, Mary Brookes, Mickey (June) McCaffrey, Chrystos, Dix, Shirl Reynolds, Maike Engelbrecht, David Maelzer, Bruce Hillier, Tova Fox, Sarah Davidson, Lisa McArthur, Susanda Yee, Judy Newman, Lee Maelzer, Chea Villanueva, Yukie Thompson, Libby Este for research and emotional support. All of my friends for being so understanding when I didn't return your phone calls for millions of years. Dianne Whelan for inspiration, friendship and the cover photo.

Richard Banner for helping me through billions of computer nightmares, whenever I asked, even interrupting your own work to do so. barbara findlay for answering legal questions. Jacquie Buncel for editorial suggestions. Rosamund Elwin and Carol Allain for publishing my first short story in *Getting Wet*. *Angles*, Vancouver's gay, lesbian and bisexual newspaper for publishing *The Beautiful Woman*, a continuing story which ran for almost five years.

Nym Hughes and Sarah Davidson for letting me stay in the a-frame where I started writing many of these stories. Silva Tennenbein for reading my chart and urging me to write. Louise Orieux and Chantal Thompson for modelling for the cover — you both look fabulous. Susan Stewart for the author photo. Sarah Leavitt for loaning me your Star of David earring. Trigger and the Lotus Club for hosting dyke readings. Flatbed for late afternoon story conferences.

My parents, Jack and Marion, for helping me with Yiddish words, songs and phrases. My Zayde Berel, olev hashalom, for telling me his stories. My Bubbe Mary for being yourself. Harvey M. Tulchinsky, olev hashalom, for all the gifts he gave me. All of the dyke writers who came before me and had the guts to be honest.

And anyone else I may have forgotten...

Contents

▼▼▼

A Different Kind of Love

▼   Last Saturday, I decided it's time to go and visit my daughter, Nomi. Six months ago she moved all the way to California — across the continent. Of course I was upset. Isn't it only natural a mother should want her daughter living close by her? She's a good girl. My husband Harry, may he rest in peace, died over a year ago. Nomi was so good to me then, watched over me like a mother watches her baby, so worried I would crack under the pressure. The boys did their best too, Izzy and Joshua, my sons. They would check on me, make sure I had groceries in the house, shovel the driveway, cut the grass, take out the trash. Anyway, I barely noticed who was there and who wasn't. For a whole year I was in a crazy fog. Like a dream. I barely slept. How could I get into bed without my Harry? For twenty-nine years I slept with the same man, in the same bed. He was part of me. When he turned over, I turned over. When he got up, I got up. When he fell asleep, I fell asleep. For twenty-nine years he snored. Bad sinuses. Drove me crazy. Kept me up half the night.

"You're snoring Harry," I'd say, nudging him with my elbow.

"Yeah. Yeah," he'd mumble. For a minute or two, the snoring would stop. Then he'd start again. I'm telling you.

Every night, for twenty-nine years, he drove me crazy with the snoring. The funny thing is, now I miss the sound.

After he died I couldn't bring myself to get into our bed. I wandered the house half the night. When I got tired, I'd go and sit in the den, on the old brown Laz-Y-Boy where Harry used to sit. I'd turn on the TV and stare past it, while the late show played. All the old movies — Bing Crosbie, Fred Astaire, Judy Garland, Debbie Reynolds, Shirley Temple, Bette Davis. I don't remember any of them. The TV kept me company. It was too quiet in the house. Who could stand such silence? Four, five in the morning I'd be asleep in the chair. When I woke up, the daytime shows would already be playing. Soap operas, talk shows, Sally Jessy, Joan Rivers, Oprah, Geraldo. All kinds of mishegus. You wouldn't believe the problems some people have.

I was a zombie. Everybody worried about me. I couldn't really hear or see. Like I was all wrapped up in cotton batting, head to toe. People talked to me, I know. I saw their mouths moving. But to tell you the truth, I didn't hear a word they said. And when I did hear, I didn't care. Believe me, I meant no offense. It's just that I wasn't expecting my husband to die. Before the heart attack, Harry was a healthy man and — I never would admit this before but, he was even a little younger than me. A couple of months. After he was gone, I didn't know how to cope. Some mornings, I barely had the strength to lift my head off the pillow. All I know is I hung on. My sister Rhoda, God bless her, called every day.

"Faygie. How are you?"

"How should I be?"

"Did you sleep?"

"Who can sleep any more?"

"Did you take your sleeping pills?"

"Who can be bothered?"

I didn't want sleeping pills. I wanted my Harry. Only fifty-four years old when he died. A young man. Why did God take him from me so soon?

"Faygie. I'm coming over after lunch."

"Don't come over. I'm fine."

"I'm coming over."

"So? Come over." Rhoda meant well, but there was nothing she could do. The only thing that would make me feel better was if she could bring my Harry back, and since she couldn't do that, I didn't care who came over and who didn't.

A year went by so fast I barely noticed. Suddenly it was time for Harry's unveiling. It was like the funeral all over again. We stood by his stone in the cemetery, a bitter cold February morning. My feet were frozen solid. The wind whipped through my coat, inside my ears and nose. I had a kerchief on my head, tied around my neck, a heavy one. The frost went right through it. My youngest son, Joshua, stood on one side, holding me up with his arm. Nomi was on the other side and Izzy, my other son, beside her. I had my black purse over my arm. It was heavy. Who knows what I had in there? I stared straight ahead as the rabbi spoke. A whole year had gone by and it felt like one day. I realized I was saying goodbye to Harry for the last time. The pain in my heart could have choked a horse. I wanted to die. I wanted God to come down and take me too, take me to my Harry. I wanted to lie down beside him just once more. I didn't care who was looking and who wasn't — I started to cry. It was a good thing Joshua and Nomi were holding me up. Otherwise, I would have collapsed on the ground.

After the service, Izzy took me to his car. We were all going back to Rhoda's house. Apparently, she decided to fix a spread, a luncheon buffet, and invite everyone over. Bagels and cream cheese, lox, salads, Rhoda's little crunchy brownies, which she claims is a secret recipe my mother, may she rest in peace, told only to my sister, which I can't imagine, because when we were kids, Rhoda never had the slightest interest in cooking. I was the one who always helped in the kitchen. Anyway, if she says my mother gave her a secret recipe, who am I to argue?

I almost slipped twice on the way to the car. Ice everywhere. I could feel the cold right through the soles of my boots. When we finally got to the parking lot, a man my age was standing by Izzy's car, clapping his hands together to keep warm. Nice looking. A pleasant smile. No hat. The wind was blowing his hair around. It was longer on one side than the other. I could see he usually combed it over to cover a bald spot. Harry, thank God, had all his hair right to the end, thick, curly and grey. The man smiled and walked over to us.

"Hello. Can you help me son?" he called out to Izzy, motioning to a car with its hood up. "Do you have cables?"

"Sure," my son said. "Just a minute. Ma, why don't you get in the car?"

The man looked over at me. "I'm sorry. Forgive me." He stuck out his hand. I gave him mine. He was wearing thick black leather gloves. "My name is Murray. Murray Feinstein."

"Hello," I said. "I'm Faygie Rabinovitch. This is my son Izzy."

"Here, let me help you." Mr. Feinstein opened the car door. He held my arm under the elbow as I got in.

"Thank you." I sat down slowly. My back was aching from standing in the cold. My heart was wide open with thoughts of Harry. Even with a kerchief, my hair was a mess from the wind. My eyes were red and puffy. I must have looked a sight. I reached up to brush a strand of loose hair from my eyes.

"My pleasure," he said with a crooked smile. His blue eyes sparkled and I blushed. It was a crazy thought, but for a minute it seemed like he was flirting with me. Even in the cold I could feel my cheeks burn. He closed the door and walked around to the front of the car. Izzy had the hood up already. I sat inside, listening to their voices, the crunch of snow under their feet, mechanical sounds as they fiddled with the motor. I could see their hands through the crack where the hood was up. I looked at Murray's black gloves. The same kind Harry used to wear. Thick leather with big seams on the side of each finger.

Sitting in the cold car, waiting, I thought about the first time I saw Harry at my cousin Herbie's bar mitzvah. Harry was older than the other boys at our table. While they told disgusting jokes, dared each other to see who could blow the biggest bubbles in their soda pop and burp the loudest, Harry quietly ate his meal and gazed at me from across the table. I was too shy to talk to him and I guess, so was he, but Rhoda kept teasing, whispering in my ear that he was sweet on me.

"Err hot aygen far dir," Rhoda assured me in Yiddish. "He has eyes for you." I remembered the way I felt the first time Harry looked at me — all fluttery inside. Of course, it turned out Rhoda was right.

What made me think about that?

I saw Mr. Feinstein get into his car and start the motor. He smiled at Izzy. My son beamed. Mr. Feinstein stepped back out of his car, said something to Izzy and they shook hands.

"Who's that?" Nomi asked when she opened the back door and slid inside.

"His name is Mr. Feinstein," I said, liking the sound of it.

"Oh yeah," said Joshua, who got in beside Nomi. "Michael Feinstein's father. His mother died in October."

When we got to Rhoda's house, Mark, her son, was shovelling the driveway. His younger sister Rachel was helping with a small red child's shovel. Izzy pulled the car up into an empty space on the street. He was helping me walk, his hand under my arm, when I felt someone behind me. I turned to look. I'm telling you, I almost had a heart attack. There was Murray Feinstein, big as life, standing on Rhoda's driveway smiling. He raised a hand and waved at me.

"Did your car break down again?" I asked.

"Not exactly." He looked down at his shoes. A nice pair. Brown leather. I could tell he had something on his mind.

I looked at Izzy. He was grinning like he had a big secret. Nomi frowned at Mr. Feinstein like she didn't trust him. Joshua went over to see his cousins.

"Mrs. Rabinovitch," Mr. Feinstein said. "The truth is I followed you here."

"You what?"

He turned to Nomi and Izzy. "Do you kids mind if I have a moment alone with your mother?"

Izzy shrugged his shoulders. "That okay with you Ma?"

Nomi stared at Murray.

I thought about it. "Sure. Why not? I'd like to hear what Mr. Feinstein has to say."

I stood in the snow on the driveway while my son and daughter went inside. The other kids were down at the end, near the street, finishing up. I looked over at the house. My sister Rhoda was standing in the window, watching. I turned back to Murray Feinstein.

"Mrs. Rabinovitch..."

"Please...call me Faygie."

"Okay. Faygie. I...I'm not very good at this. Uh. My wife died. A few months ago. I was visiting her grave today. I...well, I was wondering if perhaps, one day, that is if you would like to — if you would care to have a cup of coffee with me?"

"Mr. Feinstein!" I stared at the man. This was my husband's unveiling. My final farewell to the man I married.

"Please, call me Murray."

"Mr. Feinstein. Are you asking me out on a date?"

He nodded his head slowly. "Yes Faygie. I am."

"Mr. Feinstein," I paused. "Murray. This is my husband's unveiling."

"Yes, I know."

"Well, I don't think it's appropriate at all."

"You don't?"

"Do you?"

"I don't know. I mean, the last time I asked a lady out was thirty years ago and I married her."

God only knows what the two of us looked like, standing on Rhoda's frozen driveway. I was acting stern with him, but I didn't really mean it. I wasn't angry. I was flattered. My heart was racing in my chest. I felt happy and alive for the first time in a year. I wanted to say yes. I wanted to go out and have a little cup of coffee. What's so terrible? He seemed like a nice man. But it was wrong to be making a date on a day like this. Then I thought, maybe if I had a sign from God, or from Harry, then it would be alright. It could be anything. I was getting cold, but I didn't want to go inside just yet. Then as God is my witness, I got my sign.

Out of the blue, Murray started quietly singing the words to Harry's favourite song, and just like Harry, he stretched his arms out to the sides and puffed out his chest — a regular Tony Bennett.

You got to give a little, take a little, and let your poor heart break a little. That's the story of, that's the glory of love.

What Murray was thinking I don't know. Maybe for a minute he felt like Fred Astaire, but right there on Rhoda's driveway he started tapping his feet like a vaudeville dancer.

You got to laugh a little, cry a little, until the clouds roll by a little. That's the story of, that's the glory of love.

Then, you wouldn't believe it. He tipped his hat and held out his hand, as if we were at a bar mitzvah and he was asking me to dance. Right there, on the driveway. So? I danced a few steps with him and I even laughed a little when he twirled me under his arm.

As long as there's the two of us, we've got the world and all its charms. And when the world is through with us, we've got each other's arms.

He twirled me again, and if that wasn't enough, he went down on one knee for the finish.

You got to win a little, lose a little, and always have the blues a little. That's the story of, that's the glory of love.

We both stopped to catch our breath. We were laughing. It sounds crazy, but for a moment I felt like a young woman. I was smiling so wide, I thought my face would break.

"So how about it Faygie?" he stood up. "Just one little cup of coffee. What's it going to hurt? What's so wrong we should enjoy ourselves a little? After all, isn't that what life's all about?"

I looked into his eyes. How did he know to sing that song? I turned from him and looked up. "Thank you

Harry," I said quietly, so Murray couldn't hear. "Okay." I turned back. "One cup."

"Yes?"

"Why not?"

I don't want to brag, but you should have seen the smile on his face. Like he was the happiest man alive.

"Thank you Faygie. Thank you." He turned to leave. I caught his arm.

"So? As long as you're here already, why don't you come inside and have some lunch?"

"Thank you." He smiled even wider. You would have thought he just won the Nobel Prize. We turned around and headed up the driveway. In the living room window I saw my sister Rhoda, her husband Stanley, my friend Irma, her friend Molly, her husband Joe, my son Izzy and my daughter Nomi. All watching.

A week later Murray came by the house and picked me up. We went to Bagel Deli on Bathurst Street. We talked. He bought me coffee and a piece of cheesecake. We had a nice time. Later, he took me home and kissed me on the cheek at the door. I felt young. It was nice. We went out again the following week. He took me to a show, a nice comedy. I was so excited I can't even remember what it was called. Then, the next weekend he invited me to his nephew's wedding. He got all dressed up in a tuxedo. Even brought me flowers. So? What the heck. I've been seeing him ever since. He's very polite. Never pressures me. Always picks up the check, opens the door, helps me on with my coat. We go and see a show, have some dinner, maybe a little coffee and a donut. I don't know what'll happen between us, but in the meantime, life goes on.

So, now I'm going to visit my daughter Nomi. She

moved to San Francisco, of all places, a few months ago with her girlfriend Moonstone. Or is it Sapphire? I can never remember. They're lesbians. There. I said it. I'm not comfortable with the word, but Nomi says that's what I should call her. It doesn't bother me that she likes girls. If she's happy, I'm happy. I'm an easy-going person. I think the word bothers me more than anything. In my day, to call someone a lesbian was an insult. Now? Things are different, my daughter tells me. They even use the word on the six o'clock news. Gays this, lesbians that. How can that be? The world changes so much in a person's lifetime. I can't keep up. All my kids keep me on my toes. My sons are both a little crazy too. Maybe it runs in the family. Joshua plays guitar in a rock and roll band. For a living yet.

"What kind of a living is that for a nice Jewish boy?" I ask him.

"Ma don't worry," he tells me. "One day I'll be famous. You'll see my videos on MTV." I didn't even know what this MTV was until he explained. He's a nice boy, but sometimes I hardly recognize him with his wild haircuts.

Izzy, my middle son, is a dreamer. He tells me he's going to invent something important. An inventor? What kind of a life is that? His apartment is filled with junk. Old tires, wires, pieces of radios, TVs, things I don't even recognize. Last time I went for a visit, halfway up the stairs in his building, I heard a big bang. I was so worried, I ran the rest of the way. Believe me, I was out of breath by the time I got there.

"Don't worry Ma. I'm okay," he said as he opened the door.

"What kind of okay is this?" I asked him. His face covered in soot. Smoke everywhere. "What are you trying to do? Go to an early grave?!"

"Ma it's nothing. I just need to work out a few little kinks, but I'm going to invent the world's first biodegradable condom."

Some people might have been shocked. Me, I'm an open-minded person. If there's one thing I've learned about being a mother, it's that your kids will do whatever they want, no matter what you say. So? I leave them to their business. Especially now they're all grown up. They have their own lives. Who am I to say what makes them happy?

All my life I've trusted my feelings. For some reason last Saturday, the second I woke up, I thought about Nomi and wanted to see her. So? I called a travel agent and booked a ticket to San Francisco. Then I called Nomi and told her I was coming. "Just for a week," I said, "then I'll be out of your hair."

"Ma, please don't start with me. You can stay two weeks if you want."

To tell you the truth I'm a little nervous. You wouldn't believe it, but I've never been in my daughter's home. When she lived nearby, she always came to me. I admit it. I've always been a little scared to go to her house. I don't know what lesbians do. I know it's crazy. She's my daughter. I changed her diapers. What's to be scared of? But in my day, we called it queer. It was a terrible thing. Nowadays it seems all the young people are turning out gay.

So, here I am, on an airplane to California. I never travelled alone like this before. Always when I went somewhere, it was with Harry. Izzy drove me to the airport this morning. I asked him to pick me up early, so I'd get a window seat. I have a nice young man next to me. He has short hair, a neatly trimmed moustache, and like Joshua, an earring in his left ear. I think maybe he's in a rock band too, but after we talk a little, I find out he's a travel agent.

"I work right on the Castro," he says, as if I'm supposed to know what that means. The only Castro I ever heard of is Fidel.

He talks a lot about "his partner."

"In the travel business?" I ask.

"Oh no. He's in show business."

I think about that for a minute. "So, if he's in show business and you're in the travel business, how can he be your partner?"

"Oh honey," he waves his hand in the air. "That's how come we've stayed together for eight years. I work days and he works nights. It's perfect."

I don't know what he is talking about, but he talks so much it makes me tired. The flight is long. They serve breakfast. Not bad. Eggs, with a piece of ham, I think. In my house, I keep kosher, but once in a while I go out to a restaurant and on an airplane, I don't want to make a fuss. So? I'm not used to ham. To tell you the truth, it tastes a little like Montreal smoke meat. After breakfast they play a movie. For five dollars you can rent headphones. Who needs a movie? If I want to see a movie, I'll go to a theatre. Today, I'm going to California. Every now and then I peek at the movie anyway, without the sound. It's called *Philadelphia*, with Tom Hanks. He looks like a nice young man in the beginning of the picture, but later on, he gets very sick. Must be cancer. I'm glad I didn't pay to hear the sound. I got enough to think about. The closer we get to San Francisco, the more nervous I feel. I don't know what I expect to find. Nomi's been seeing this girl Sapphire for two years. Never once did I meet her.

"Bring her to supper," I told Nomi.

"We're not ready for that yet Ma, but thanks for asking."

"What's to get ready?"

"We're just getting to know each other. I'm not ready to introduce her to my family."

"Alright," I gave in, "only don't say I never asked."

Now, finally I'm going to meet my daughter's girlfriend and I'm nervous. I don't know why. What could be so frightening? What do I think? Wild sex orgies in the kitchen? Nomi tells me their love is no different than if they were a man and a woman. So? I should have an open mind, right?

At the airport I look around for Nomi. It's crowded. People rush by. Travellers with bags, people being picked up, pilots in uniform, stewardesses shlepping bags on little folding wheels. I see the young man who was sitting beside me on the plane run into the arms of another young man. They kiss. On the lips. Like sweethearts. I suddenly realize he's a faygela, like my Nomi. Who would have known? He looks like anybody else.

I don't want to get lost, so I stand in one place near the gate. Nomi is late. Maybe she got stuck in traffic. Who knows? The airport is more hectic than in Toronto. Every few minutes an announcement comes over the loudspeaker. A woman standing beside me lights a cigarette. I can tell by the strong smell it's American. A little boy runs around her legs in circles with his arms spread out like wings. He's making noises from his throat like an airplane. I reach in my purse for my Craven A's and light one. I start to wonder. Maybe I'm standing in the wrong place. Maybe I should find a phone and call Nomi. Maybe something went wrong.

"Ma!" I hear my daughter's voice from behind.

"Nomi, mamelah. You look wonderful. Let me see you."
I stand back a minute to have a look on her. She looks healthy and happy. Her hair's shorter than the last time I saw her. She's wearing blue jeans, a button down shirt,

heavy black boots. Like a young boy. Sometimes, it surprises me. But, I don't say a word. After all, who am I to judge?

She bends down and we hug. She seems taller than the last time I saw her, but maybe it's me. Maybe I'm shrinking. It can happen. My mother, may she rest in peace, shrunk five inches before she died.

"Ma. You look great." She holds my hands and stands back a bit to look at me. "You look different. What happened?"

"What do you mean what happened? Nothing happened. Everything's the same."

She looks at me sceptically. "No. Something's different." She smiles. "Are you still seeing that man? What's his name?"

"Who? You mean Murray?"

"Who?" she mocks me. "What do you mean who? How many men are you seeing?"

"Stop Nomi. Please. Okay. I'm still seeing him. Is that so terrible?"

"Terrible? No, Ma. It's wonderful." Nomi picks up my small travel bag. "Come on. Your suitcase will be at the baggage area." She takes my arm and steers me to the right.

With my suitcase, we go outside to find her car.

"It's very beautiful here," I say as we drive to her house. The sky is bright blue and the sun is shining. We pass palm trees and bushes I've never seen before. Some are flowering, with bright red, purple and orange blooms. The houses are lovely, well-kept, old Victorian style, all painted fancy shmancy in different colours. I keep seeing the same striped flag sticking out of windows and on porches. All different coloured stripes.

"What's with the coloured flags?" I ask. "I don't think I've seen a flag like that before."

"It's the gay flag Ma."

"What?"

"It's the rainbow flag. It stands for gay pride. People hang it to show it's a gay household."

"Right outside like that? Why do they have to announce it to the whole world?"

"Why not? There's nothing to be ashamed of. It's not gay people who have a problem. It's the rest of the world. What do you want? You want I should hide who I am!?" My daughter is passionate. When she gets on a topic she reminds me of her father. When Harry was mad about something in politics, he would rant and rave. His face would turn all red. The veins would be popping out of his neck.

"Cool down Harry," I'd say to him, "remember your blood pressure."

"I was only asking," I say to my daughter. "Calm down."

A few minutes later, we pull up in front of a tall house at the top of a steep road. States Street. Just up the hill from the street called Castro, where the young man from the plane said he works. The trim on Nomi's house is purple, yellow and pink, and to my surprise, sticking out from a window on the second floor is a gay flag.

"Oy, Nomi. At your house too?" I can't hide my shock as I stare at the flag. "What about the neighbours? Do you have any trouble with them?"

"What? Oh you mean the flag?" She laughs. "Ma don't worry, half the street is gay."

"No kidding?" I get out of the car and look around at her neighbours' houses to see if they look unusual. Next door on a tiny lawn stands a green bush with bright red flowers that remind me of the ends of brushes. The house is nicely kept, a fresh paint job in three different shades of lavender. We pass a sewer grate on the street and a rotten smell drifts into my nose, mixing with the fresh, sweet scent of a huge pink geranium bush, big like I've never seen before, on Nomi's tiny front lawn. A block down, some workers are fixing the road. A jackhammer vibrates in my ears. Such a noise. As we climb the stairs to the front porch, I notice the fog blocking the sun. The air feels cold. Nomi opens the front door and I follow her up a steep flight of stairs.

Inside doesn't seem strange at all. There's a living room to the left of the stairs with a couch, some plants, a big armchair and pictures on the wall. So far, so good. There's a hallway leading to the back. Beyond the living room, I can see the kitchen.

"Come on Ma, I'll introduce you to Sapphire."

I follow Nomi across the room. I hate to admit it, but my heart is beating a little too fast at the thought of finally meeting this girl. I'm a little worried, if I don't calm down, maybe I'm going to have a heart attack.

Standing by the stove, stirring something in a pot, is a nice looking young woman. Very feminine. I'm surprised. After Nomi and her mannish hairstyles all these years, I was expecting her girlfriend to look even more like a man. If I saw her on the street, I'd never know she was a lesbian. She turns around and smiles at me.

"Ma, this is Sapphire."

She holds out her hand and I shake it.

"Welcome to our home Mrs. Rabinovitch," she says to me. "Would you like a cup of tea or a cold glass of ginger ale?" Nomi must have told her what I like to drink.

"A nice cup of tea, if it's not too much trouble dear." I sit at the table to rest my legs. There are so many hills in San

Francisco, even to walk from the car to the house is like climbing a mountain.

"Hi babe," Nomi goes over to her girlfriend. She puts both arms around her waist, hugs her tight and kisses her on the lips. Sapphire strokes my daughter's face and gives her a long look like you'd see on a bride's face just before she kisses the groom. It seems so natural. For a minute, I forget I'm not used to it.

After the tea, Nomi shows me around. At the back of the apartment is the master bedroom, which she calls "our bedroom." The bathroom is the old-fashioned kind, with a toilet all by itself in a small room and a sink and an old claw-foot bathtub in a larger room next to it. At the other end of the flat, overlooking the street, is a smaller bedroom with a double bed, a desk with a computer, a book shelf, some pens and notebooks.

"This is Sapphire's office," she says, "but we also use it as a guest room."

"Her office? Well, Nomi. I don't want to put her out. I'll sleep in the living room. After all, I've been sleeping in the den since your father died. I'm used to it."

"Ma. It's fine. We discussed it. You'll sleep in here."

I go over to the window to look out. Down the street where we parked the car a bus drives past. Then a motorcycle. Two young boys on skateboards race down the middle of the road.

"Doesn't she need to work in here?" I know from my daughter her girlfriend edits textbooks for a living.

"I'm going to move her computer into the dining room. We just didn't have time before. It's been a hectic week."

"Please Nomi. I don't want you girls to go to so much trouble."

"It's no trouble Ma. It's settled. You're staying in here."
She unplugs the computer and picks it up.

"Careful, mamelah. You'll hurt your back." I stay in the
guest room, unpacking my things. I have a couple of blouses
I don't want to wrinkle, so I hang them in the closet. There's
a lot of noise from the street. Every few minutes a bus goes
by. People honk their horns. Kids yell. There must be a
school nearby. I lie down and close my eyes. Just for a little
while. When I wake up I feel better, so I walk down the hall
to the living room. Nomi is sitting in a big armchair, her
friend standing behind her, rubbing her shoulders. Sometimes Nomi looks so much like her father it shocks me. I
remember when I used to stand behind Harry like that.

"Come on in Ma," Nomi says when she sees me in the
doorway.

"I don't want to interrupt anything...."

"Ma. What's to interrupt? Sapphire's giving me a mas-
sage. I pulled a muscle."

"That's the best thing then." I sit on the couch.

"Sapphire's cooking tonight Ma. She's making home-
made burritos. Do you know what they are?"

"Nomi, please." I give my daughter a look and then
wink at her friend. "I may be old, but I wasn't born yesterday. Once in a while your father used to take me to a
Mexican restaurant downtown."

After dinner I tell the girls I'm tired and go to my room.
I feel a little funny about seeing my daughter with this girl.
They hold hands and touch a lot. Not any more than any
newlyweds I've seen, but I'm just not used to seeing two
girls together like that. I get ready for bed and crawl under
the covers to read a book. I picked up a new bestseller at the
airport. I like a good murder mystery now and then. Takes

my mind off my own troubles. I doze off. Something wakes me. Shouting on the street.

"You stole my leather jacket!" a man's yelling. "You hear me? While I was sleeping. I'll get you for this, you bastard. I'll find you. That's my jacket, you bastard!"

I slip out of bed and tip toe to the window, where I pull the drape aside, just enough to see through. A man with long blonde hair tied in a pony-tail stands in the middle of the road. He's swaying, like he's drunk. A car drives by and honks its horn. Misses him by inches.

"Fuck you!" he screams and puts his middle finger high in the air. "Fuck all of you!" I don't like that kind of language, but even from upstairs I'm not going to fight with a drunken man. I close the curtain and get back into bed. I doze for a while. Then I wake to the sound of another bus. I hear young boys on skateboards, but I must be dreaming. The clock says five a.m. Who would ride a skateboard at that hour?

At seven o'clock I get up and go into the kitchen. Since I can't sleep, I might as well cook breakfast. I find a cast iron frying pan hanging on a hook on the wall. Before Nomi or her friend are awake, I start to fix up a batch of potato latkes.

"Ma. What are you doing up so early cooking?" Nomi walks into the room in her housecoat.

"Shah. What's so terrible? I'm making a little breakfast is all. Potato latkes." I don't want to tell Nomi I couldn't sleep. She'll only worry.

"Potato latkes! I haven't had any in ages." Nomi sits at the table. "So tell me Ma. What do you think of Sapphire? You haven't said a word yet."

"She seems very nice dear. Very feminine. I never would have thought...."

"What were you expecting Ma?"

"Well, you know. I thought she'd be...different." I open a cupboard below the sink and find a big bag of potatoes.

"You mean you thought she'd be more butch?"

"Well, if that's what you call it." I pick out six medium sized potatoes and put them in the sink.

Nomi laughs. "I guess I'm more the butch Ma."

"Is that how it goes Nomi? One of you is like the man and the other is like the woman?" I turn on the tap and begin to scrub the potatoes.

"No Ma, not exactly. We're both women. But you know I've always been butch in my style."

"Such a funny word. I'm not used to it. Is that how all the gay girls are Nomi? One's...butch and the other's feminine?"

"No. Not all. It used to be that way, back in the fifties. But these days, you can be whoever you want. Some couples are both femme or both butch. Some lesbians are...just androgynous."

"An...what?" Half the time I don't know what my daughter is talking about. But I have to ask. Right? How else am I going to learn? "Where's your grater Nomi?"

"Androgynous," she repeats. "It means a little bit of both masculine and feminine. Lots of lesbians are like that. We have a cuisenart, Ma." She points to the machine sitting in a corner on the counter. "Why don't you use that?"

"Why? Because I've been grating by hand for thirty years. It's always worked before. Why should I switch now?"

She laughs and stands up. "Okay. Let me see if I can find a grater." She rummages in the cupboards. Meanwhile I throw a little oil into the frying pan and open a cupboard over the sink. I find a box of matzah meal and a can of baking powder. The salt is already out. "You have eggs?"

"Here we go." She hands me a grater. "Yeah, in the fridge." She opens the door and pulls out a dozen brown eggs. "Ma. I'm glad you came. It means a lot to me for you to know about my life."

"I'm your mother," I say, as I start to grate into a big stainless steel bowl. "Why shouldn't I want to know?"

"You'd be surprised Ma. Lots of my friends don't have mothers like you. Some of them won't even talk to their kids because they're gay. Some are never allowed in their parents' home again. Well, Sapphire for example. When she told her parents, they freaked. She hasn't seen them or spoken to them in five years."

"No. It can't be so. How could a mother do that to her daughter? The poor kid. That's shameful." I stop grating for a minute. I admit it. Sometimes I don't understand my daughter. Lots of the time she shocks me, but never once did I think to disown her. Harry too. And he was always more old-fashioned than me. Oh, he'd carry on, scream and shout when his kids did strange things, but he'd always come around in the end. He never stopped loving his children, no matter how foolish he thought they were.

"Nomi. Is it true?" I continue grating. "Her parents don't speak to her at all?"

"Yeah Ma, it's true."

I feel a stab of pain in my heart. Not just for the girl, but for myself. My mother was a hard woman. She never liked Harry. She wanted me to marry a rich man — a doctor, a lawyer, a businessman. But I fell in love with Harry, a poor boy from a poor family. The first time I brought him home my mother gave him the third degree. When she found out he was a painter, an artist, she hit the roof.

"If you marry this dreamer, you'll live a life of misery," she said. Right in front of Harry. "How will he support you?

Don't expect any help from me, Faygie, if you marry this nothing."

My father tried to calm her down, but it was no use. My mother was a headstrong woman. She cried at my wedding, tears of remorse. Never once did she say a kind word to Harry. Never once. Okay, we never lived like millionaires, but we never starved either. A few of his paintings sold. When the money wasn't there he sold stereos at Sears. His old friend Myer was head of the department. When Harry needed the work, Myer would hire him. My husband was a good man, and my own mother couldn't see it.

Here I am, thirty years later, looking into the face of my daughter. I realize I could repeat my mother's mistake. Until my mother's death, I lived with her disappointment in me and in Harry. How could I do the same thing to my daughter? I never forgave my mother, and I was never close to her again. I don't want my only daughter to feel that way about me. So, she loves a woman? So, her girlfriend has a crazy name? So, she comes from a different background? When I look in Nomi's eyes, I see her love for this girl. When I clear my head and really look, I see how happy she is. And when I think of the pain in my own heart for all the years my mother refused to accept my Harry, I know there's only one thing to do. I turn to my daughter.

"Well, it's settled then," I say, as I add half a cup of matzah meal to my potatoes.

"What's settled Ma?" Nomi looks at me with her big brown eyes.

"Your girlfriend can call me Ma. She's young yet, and I can see how happy you are with her. If her own parents can't see what a lovely girl she is, then she can think of me as her Ma." When I look again at my daughter's face, there are tears in her eyes. "Mamelah, what's a matter? Why are you so sad?"

She stands up and puts her arms around me. "Ma, you're the greatest."

"Never mind." I pat her back gently. "I'm your mother. I love you. Anyhow, neither of your brothers are getting married so fast. She'll be my first daughter-in-law. Am I right?"

"Course you're right Ma. Wait here, I'm going to tell Sapphire."

"Wait here? Where would I go?" She runs out of the room to wake her girlfriend.

I stand by the stove, spoon batter into the sizzling oil and try to imagine how a mother could shut out her own daughter like that. Then I get to thinking about Murray Feinstein. I still haven't told him about Nomi. After all, we've only been dating a few months. I wonder how he would take the news. Sometimes it's hard to tell with people, even if you think you know them. One thing's for sure. If Murray can't take it, then goodbye. There's more men where he came from, but I only got one daughter. I don't care how crazy her ideas are, she's still my little girl. And anyway, when you get right down to it, what's so bad about it? Some people would criticize me for going out with Murray so soon after Harry's death. Other people wouldn't understand Nomi's love for Sapphire. But when I see my daughter look into the eyes of her girlfriend, I see myself when I first fell in love with Harry. It's just a different kind of love. That's all.

▼ ▼ ▼

In Her Nature

▼   Barbara Anna Silverstein should have been a boy.
Everybody thought so. Her mother, her father, her sister, her
brother, her teacher, all the other kids at school, even Doctor
Pearlman.

"Occasionally, this happens," he explained to Gloria and
Phil Silverstein, as Barbara sat on a black vinyl loveseat in
the waiting room, playing World War Two fighter pilots
with her Barbie and Ken dolls. Beside her, a woman was
reading about Apollo 7's orbit around the earth in *Life*
magazine, puffing on a Virginia Slims 100's, flicking ashes
into a stainless steel floor ashtray. She had long, bleached
blonde hair parted in the middle. Her striped skirt was
fashionably short, a wide black belt rode low on her hips.
Frank Sinatra's voice flowed from a small eight track player
on the nurse's desk, singing his new hit, "Something Stupid." The nurse wore a starched white uniform with a little
white cap and answered a big, black rotary telephone. Her
backcombed hair puffed up like Barbara Eden in "I Dream
Of Jeannie." From the corner of her eye, she watched Barbara hold the dolls high above her head and, complete with
sound effects, pretend they were jet plane bombers hurtling
through the atmosphere at astronomical speeds. Poised opposite each other, they crashed in the air, causing an explosion

that reverberated through the entire waiting room, then tumbled to tragic deaths on the faded orange carpet.

"In rare cases," Dr. Pearlman lectured Barbara's perturbed parents, "a child is born with the wrong set of secondary sex characteristics."

"Huh?" said Phil.

"Shah, Phil. Let Dr. Pearlman finish," said his wife.

"Anatomically speaking, Barbara has all the correct physical attributes for a girl, yet she displays personality characteristics generally seen in boys."

"Oh my god," said Gloria, clutching her navy blue handbag tightly in her lap.

Phil took a breath, loosened his wide, flowered tie, sighed deeply and reached for the pack of Viceroys in his shirt pocket. He was a busy man with a store to run. He wished the doctor would get to the damn point. It was Gloria's idea to come here. He didn't see any big deal. So his youngest daughter liked to play baseball more than she liked to play dolls. So she liked to climb trees. So she hated wearing dresses and liked to run around in jeans and t-shirts. She was only a little kid. She'd grow out of it.

"Is it some kind of sickness Doc? Is that what you're saying?" Phil slid a cigarette from the pack, slipped it between his lips and in a graceful, practised manner of long habit, flicked his Zippo lighter on his pants and ignited the flame.

The doctor smiled condescendingly at Phil, "It's more like a hormonal problem."

Phil scowled, inhaled and exhaled deeply.

"Well...is there a cure Dr. Pearlman?" said Gloria, fanning the smoke, annoyed at her husband.

"Well, not really, but there are treatments — therapies."

"What? You mean like a shrink? She's only eight years

old for god's sake, Gloria. We're not sending her to some head shrinker." Phil scratched his scalp. Gloria had insisted he stop James Deaning his hair with Brylcream and try a new spray — "The Dry Look." His hair looked better, but it itched.

"Mr. Silverstein," Dr. Pearlman oozed in his most patronizing tone, "I was thinking more of therapy that can be done in the home. Studies have shown that behaviourial regulation can sometimes result in modification, especially when the condition is caught so early on."

Phil looked at his watch. "Listen Doc, just write me a prescription and we'll fill it. Okay?"

The doctor laughed in a polite way that annoyed the hell out of Phil. Then he wrote a list on a prescription pad and handed it to Gloria.

"Now, I want you to follow my instructions to the letter and bring the young lady back for a visit in three months. I'll evaluate her progress at that time."

"Three months," grumbled Phil, rubbing his new sideburns as they all walked down the hall to the elevators. "Damn doctors. Think they know everything, just 'cause they made it through medical school. What's going to change in three months?"

Gloria stopped reading the doctor's instructions to fasten the buttons on her lime green midi coat and glare at her husband. A sinking feeling gripped Barbara's stomach as the elevator doors opened and the family stepped in.

After that day, life was never the same for Barbara Anna Silverstein. Gloria taped Dr. Pearlman's list on the refrigerator door. It was higher than Barbara's eye level and written in doctor scrawl. Even when she pulled a kitchen chair up to the fridge and stood on it, she couldn't read what it said. It didn't matter. She found out soon enough.

Beginning the next morning, no one called her Bobby, her nickname. They all started calling her Bar-bara. Her father's worn, brown baseball glove sat on the top shelf of the front closet gathering dust. Before the pivotal visit to Dr. Pearlman, Phil had been working with Bobby on her curve ball, teaching her to fake out the batter by putting a top right spin on the ball, just as it left her hand. Phil could see the kid was a natural. She put everything she had into her pitch. If she was a boy he'd have put her in little league, maybe even volunteered to coach a season or two. But there were no little leagues for girls. Unheard of. Phil would have considered it unfair if he'd thought about it, but he was a man who followed the fashion of his day. His daughter was going through a phase — eventually she'd be interested in girl-things like clothes, make-up and boys. It was a matter of time. To humour his wife, who was gravely distraught over Barbara's unconventional behaviour, he was willing to go along with Dr. Pearlman's instructions.

Having given in to Gloria, Phil never took a good look at Dr. Pearlman's list. But, every day, Barbara felt its ominous power loom over her life like a giant cage slowly sinking, trapping and confining her. So many things Barbara was no longer allowed to do. Not allowed to wear pants, ever. Not allowed to play cops and robbers with Tommy Shecter and his brother Leo. Not allowed to get dirty, climb trees, turn somersaults, yell, put her elbows on the table, pretend two empty thread spools were racing cars and make them crash, play World War Two fighter pilots with her dolls or imagine she was a private in the army stuck on KP duty washing dishes. When she begged to be allowed to wear jeans to school, her mother would say "What? You want everyone to think you're queer?" Barbara didn't know what queer was. She simply preferred pants to dresses.

Eventually, Barbara stopped talking. She stopped laughing, playing, running and smiling. She walked slowly with her head down, ate only when her belly hurt, ground her teeth together at night and had bad dreams. One night, she woke sweating, gasping for breath. She dreamed she was walking down the street in a flowing white Cinderella dress. It was itchy all over. Tommy Shecter ran up from behind, shoved her down on wet grass and ran away laughing, waving Dr. Pearlman's white list in the air above his head. Barbara tried desperately to get up and chase him, but every time her foot caught in the crinoline and she collapsed in the mud. All the kids from her class stood on the lawn across the street laughing at her. Her brother Joel and her father were behind, throwing a baseball back and forth. The ball became a tomato gushing red as it splattered on the ground between them. Barbara sat up in bed in a haze, half awake, half asleep, the dream still alive in her mind. Ellen, her sister, slept in the bed beside her. The shadow of her dresser wavered against the wall. The furnace in the basement groaned on with a familiar rumble. She rubbed her eyes. Her parents were arguing. Their bedroom door was part way open and she could hear clearly.

"I don't care if he's a doctor. I don't care if he's God Gloria. He's wrong," Barbara's father said.

"Phil, please. Don't you think it's breaking my heart too? She's just a little girl. She doesn't know what she wants. She'll get over it. She'll learn to like dresses and dolls. Wait, you'll see. In a few months she'll forget the whole thing. She'll be fine."

"The light is gone from her eyes, Gloria. Can't you see that?"

"What choice do we have Phil? What? You want your daughter should grow up to be 'funny'?"

Barbara's stomach fluttered when her mother said "funny." She felt ashamed. She must have done something very bad for her parents to be acting this way. Something that was a big sccret, only talked about late at night and in doctor's offices. The door to Barbara's parents' room clicked shut. Their voices became faint and muffled. Then she only heard TV sounds and Ellen's breathing. She couldn't keep her eyes open any longer.

One afternoon, Barbara's mother was drinking Maxwell House instant and blabbing on the phone. Ellen was watching "Hogan's Heroes." Joel was playing basketball in the park with his friends. And her father was at the store. Barbara was on the front steps in a powder blue skirt and blouse, watching an ant drag a bread crumb across the grey cement of the porch steps. Tommy Shecter came riding along on his bike, a brand new five-speed, metallic gold with a banana seat and monkey bars.

"Wanna play cops and robbers?" he asked.

Barbara glanced over her shoulder toward her mother and shrugged.

"Come on Bobby," Tommy begged.

Barbara checked for her mother again, then looked back at Tommy. "Okay," she agreed and ran after him, down the street and into his backyard.

They played for a long time. Tommy was the robber. He broke into the bank, stole all the money and hid. Bobby was the cop. She found a gun-shaped branch on the ground under a chestnut tree and shoved it into the belt of her skirt. Staying close to the wall of Tommy's house, Bobby crept through the night shadows of the darkened city searching for the robber. She caught a glimpse of his face hiding behind the Empire State Building, whipped her gun out from her holster, held it in front of her and yelled, "Freeze! I know you're in there. Come out with your hands up!"

"Bang!" Tommy thrust his new black cap gun between the leaves and shot her. A blast of smoke and the smell of gunpowder rose in the late afternoon air.

"You missed me," Bobby yelled.

"I got you!" screamed Tommy.

"Did not!"

"Did too!"

"Not."

"Hah! You don't even have a real gun. You just have a branch. I have a real gun. You're dead!"

Bobby didn't have an answer. Tommy was right. He did have a real gun. Hers was just pretend.

"I'm not playing!" She threw her gun to the ground and ran home. "I hate Tommy," she grumbled. "He's lucky. He's a boy. It's not fair. He doesn't have to wear stupid, dumb dresses." Barbara stomped into the house, marched into the kitchen and slumped down on a chair opposite her mother, who was still talking on the phone.

"I gotta go. I'll call you back," she heard her mother say. "Barbara Anna Silverstein!" she shouted.

Uh oh. Barbara looked up in horror.

"What have you done to your leotards?"

Barbara looked down. Both light blue knees were ripped. There was mud on one shin. She felt the blood rise in her cheeks. She shrugged.

"What were you doing?"

Barbara shrugged again.

"What do you mean you don't know?"

"Just playing."

Her mother shook her head. "You were just playing. Oy Barbara, what are we going to do with you?"

She shrugged again.

"Go and change your leotards. Put the dirty ones in the washing machine. And get me a light-bulb while you're down there."

Barbara hated her mother for making her wear stupid dresses. She hated Tommy for shooting her. She hated the basement and most of all, she hated Dr. Pearlman's dumb list on the fridge, laughing and glaring at her daily, a giant finger pointed at her, scolding.

"Okay." She hopped on each stair down to the big unfinished laundry room, with its cold cement floors, steel support beams and the huge, grey furnace that sometimes turned into a monster. Barbara peeled off her leotards and threw them in the washing machine. Stacks of cardboard boxes were piled beside the wooden storage shelves Phil had built on the far wall, where Gloria kept cans of Campbell's Soup, Kraft Dinner, Rice A Roni, Pop Tarts, Jell-o pudding and way up high, on the second from the top row a box of Nice 'N Easy hair dye, a garden hose and an orange and blue box of light bulbs. Even standing on her tip toes, Barbara couldn't quite reach the bulbs. She slid a box over.

As she climbed onto it, the cardboard sank and her foot wedged inside. She grabbed the metal shelf with one hand and lowered her free leg to the floor. When she yanked the flaps open to release her foot, something familiar caught her attention. Barbara opened the box. Her eyes grew wide. Jeans, t-shirts and runners. All the clothes her mother had taken away and hidden. A smile spread across Barbara's face. She touched her favourite blue jeans. The denim felt strong in her hands. She lifted the pants out of the box.

Barbara glanced quickly toward the stairs, then slipped into her jeans, pulling them up under her skirt. She felt just right. Covered and protected. She could run and jump again, climb trees, play with Tommy and the other boys, ride her bike, win any race. She felt like herself, like Bobby.

"Barbara!" her mother's voice pierced the silence of the basement. "Where's my light-bulb? What are you doing down there?"

"Nothing."

"Well, hurry up then."

Bobby stepped back on the box and, reaching as high as she could, grabbed a carton of sixty watt light-bulbs. She jumped down, ran out of the storage room and dashed for the stairs. Halfway up she remembered her jeans. She stopped and leaned against the wall. If her mother saw she'd found her clothes, she'd take them away again. She put the light-bulbs down on the steps and rolled her pant legs up once, twice, three times, until the pants were covered entirely by her skirt. She looked down. You could hardly tell.

"Barbara?!"

"Okay!"

Bobby hurried up the stairs and into the kitchen. She handed her mother the bulbs. Gloria looked at her and frowned.

"Fix your skirt," she said. "It's all bunched up."

Bobby smoothed the front of her skirt down as best she could. It was still pretty lumpy.

Gloria Silverstein surveyed her daughter. It was obvious she had something on under her skirt. She decided to let it go for the time being, as Bobby skipped out of the room. At least she seemed happy today.

Later that evening, while Barbara slept, Gloria quietly slipped into her bedroom. She found her daughter's blue skirt crumpled up in a ball on the floor. Inside was a pair of jeans that had been packed away in a box in the basement. Just as she thought.

"So? She's a smart kid. She figured it out," Phil said when Gloria brought the evidence into the kitchen.

"Phil! We have to do something! You heard what Dr. Pearlman said."

"Gloria. In five weeks they're opening a huge Save-On-Fruit store three blocks down. They'll murder us! They deal in volume — they can sell for less. I've finally built my father's little store up so's we actually make a profit. It's taken fifteen years to get where we are, Gloria. And now because of Save-On-Fruit, we're about to be clobbered. I've got things on my mind, bigger than what kind of clothes my kids wear."

"Phil! What good is money if your family is in crisis?"

"Who's in crisis?"

The next morning Bobby found her jeans on the floor right where she'd left them. While everyone was in the kitchen, she slipped into the pants, rolled them up and covered them with the skirt she was supposed to wear. She crept quietly into the kitchen for breakfast. Joel was stuffing Fruit Loops into his mouth, head down, face almost in his bowl. Ellen was standing by the counter waiting for toast. Gloria looked up from her morning newspaper and watched Bobby go over to the cupboard for a bowl. She could see the pants under the dress.

Bobby felt her mother's eyes. She held her breath all the way to the table with her bowl.

Gloria didn't know what to do. In a week she was supposed to take Barbara back to Dr. Pearlman. She had tried to follow his instructions, but nothing had changed. Her daughter still acted more like a boy than a girl. Maybe Phil was right. Maybe it was just in her nature.

"Thank God. All our children are healthy," he always said, as if that was enough to ask.

Maybe she was worrying over nothing. Maybe it was just a phase and Barbara would grow out of it. Gloria shook her head, sighed and drank the rest of her coffee.

"Hurry up and eat kids. You'll be late for school," she said.

Bobby bent low over her bowl, like her brother, and scooped spoonfuls of cereal into her mouth, filling her cheeks and chewing loudly. Her feet didn't reach the floor, she swung them back and forth in the air. Joel pushed his chair back, stood and brought his bowl up to his mouth, tipping his head back and draining the rest of the milk. Bobby jumped down, pushed her chair back, raised her bowl and did the same. As he grabbed his lunch bag and raced out of the house, she followed, slipping on her way down the front steps and skinning her knee.

"Hey Joel, wait for me," she yelled after him.

"Drop dead squirt."

"You wish," she yelled back. Throwing all her strength into it, she ran after him, like lightning, like an Olympic runner, like a speeding bullet, like Superman, until she was alongside her older brother, running all the way to school.

▼▼▼

Rosie's Seaside

▼ Toby Lapinsky steered her black and chrome Kawasaki 450 LTD through cold winter rain into the alley behind her apartment on East Eighth. The front tire crunched on wet gravel as she braked to a stop. She snapped out the kickstand, leaned her weight on her left foot, swung her right leg over the seat and down. Using her teeth, she removed her right glove. With wet, frozen fingers, Toby unfastened the bungie cord securing her canvas knapsack onto the rear of her seat. She trudged up the wooden fire escape, three flights to her bachelor apartment, the set of keys clipped to her belt jingled against her hip. She unlocked the door, stepped inside, tossed her gloves and knapsack on a chair and bent forward to undo the buckles on her boots.

In the kitchen, Toby lay her helmet on the table and slipped off her yellow rain slicker. Everything was drenched. Felix, her big, orange cat jumped onto the table and began to purr. Toby nuzzled her face against his forehead. She didn't usually allow him on the kitchen table, but, for the moment she was tired and cold and didn't particularly care. Still in rubber pants, she tramped down the hall to the bathroom. Felix followed, meowing angrily when she accidentally stepped on his tail. She peeled off damp clothes until she stood naked in the bathroom. Shivering, Toby turned the shower tap and waited for the water to heat up.

"Felix, out." She nudged him with her bare foot and closed the door to retain the steam. Toby showered, hot water pouring over her head and down her face, soothing her tired body. It was Friday, the end of a long week. Every muscle ached. She felt a hundred years old. November was the busiest time of year at The Alfalfa Sprout Natural Foods Co-op. All day Toby drove the fork-lift, loading and unloading trucks with organic vegetables and fruit. Toby was happy to have a unionized job with three years seniority, good wages and benefits for "same sex spouses." Though she wasn't political and didn't have a steady girlfriend, it pleased her to know that at work, at least, she had the same rights as straight people. Toby's father Harvey worked in a unionized print shop, had been there thirty years. His constant lectures on the value of unions were ingrained deep in Toby's sensibilities.

Out of the shower, Toby posed in front of the mirror, a towel tied around her waist, another draped over her shoulders. She wiped her hand over the mirror's steamy surface. A tired woman looked back at her, exhausted enough to climb into bed with a beer, pizza and the late show. But she was a single dyke on a Friday night. She didn't work this hard to waste her precious weekends watching TV and growing old alone.

In the bedroom Toby jerked open the squeaky bottom drawer of her old wooden dresser. Inside she found a white t-shirt, black leather chrome-studded wrist band, fresh blue 501's, a smooth leather belt and black socks. In the bathroom, still warm and misty from her shower, she slicked back her short wavy hair with a thick glob of gel, splashed a few drops of cologne on the back of her neck and brushed her teeth.

Outside, the rain had stopped. Toby slid into her black

leather jacket, adjusted her helmet and gloves and rode out into evening traffic.

At Rosie's Seaside Pub, Toby stood in the entrance, letting her eyes adjust to the bar. She removed her helmet and checked her hair in the mirror, the one her friend Sal Sanduchio, owner and bartender, had thoughtfully hung for just this purpose. Watching over the women who frequented Rosie's — "the girls," as she called them — came naturally to Sal. In her mid-fifties, Sal was an old style butch with closely cropped salt and pepper hair and deep brown, sad, sensitive eyes. A white t-shirt, black jeans and a leather vest covered her strong, wide body. An enormous set of keys dangled on her belt. Her Marlboro's lived in the inside pocket of her vest.

Sal was more than a bartender. She was a dyke lighthouse carefully illuminating the rocks ahead to keep her girls from running aground. If a woman was having a hard night, Sal would make her laugh, offer advice, tease and encourage her. Sal liked to act tough, yet she wasn't afraid to show her soft side. Role model, friend, adviser and comrade, she knew everybody and everybody knew her. Having once worked as a busgirl at the club, Toby was especially close to Sal.

Sal opened the bar with her lover Rosie in the late seventies. When they found the old pub on a deserted street down by the docks, they worried it was too far out of the way. The rent was cheap though, so they gambled. The only women's bar in town for most of fifteen years, Rosie's did quite well. After Rosie died, Sal was glad they'd named the club after her lover. As long as she kept the bar open and filled with women, it felt almost as if Rosie was still with her.

Nursing a bruised ego, Toby hadn't been to Rosie's for a while. Heather, the latest love of her life, had dumped her after three short weeks. Toby was always falling in love, sometimes at first sight. Trouble was, her relationships never lasted very long. Sometimes she left, more often women left her. Toby never wasted much time in grief or regret. Never more than a week or two would pass, before she'd be out there again, searching for the new Ms. Right, ever hopeful her latest fling would be The One.

A familiar rap song wound its way to Toby at the entrance of the club, mixed with muffled sounds of women talking. A large pink neon sign hummed audibly, "Welcome to Rosie's Seaside Pub." The long dark oak counter, originally constructed at the turn of the century, was well-polished and lovingly oiled once a month by Sal herself. Behind the counter, mounted high on the wall, were two deep cupboards of the same rich wood. Mirrors lined the space between. Bottles of liquor and beer were displayed on glass shelves. A large black and white poster of k.d. lang hung on the wall to the left. To the right, not surprisingly, perched a similar one of Melissa Ethridge.

"I knew you'd be back tonight," Sal announced with authority as Toby sauntered into the half-full bar, handing her helmet and jacket to Liz at the coat check.

"Hi Sal. Did ya miss me?" Toby sidled up to the bar.

"Hell no." Sal winked. "We figured you were out of town or married and living happily ever after."

Toby jammed both hands into her front pockets. "What? You mean you didn't hear the latest?"

"No, what's the latest?" Sal wiped the counter with a large wet rag.

"About me and Heather."

Sal shrugged. "No. You know me kiddo. I keep my nose clean. Stay out of other people's business."

Toby snickered. "Yeah right. So what did you hear? What's everybody saying?"

Sal sighed and looked at Toby tenderly. "Didn't she tell you?"

"Tell me what?"

Sal sighed again. "What did Heather tell you?"

Toby winced and blew a stream of air out the side of her mouth. "Same shit we all tell each other. You know. Not ready to commit. Needs her space. You know."

Sal sighed. "Don't take it hard Tobe okay? After all, you were only with her what? Couple a weeks?"

"Almost a month. What? Tell me?"

"You should ask her yourself, but I'm pretty sure I saw her with someone else."

"That bitch!" Toby threw one hand up in the air. "Damn sheets aren't even cold yet."

"Come on Tobe. Let it go. You'll find someone else soon and I betcha she'll be even better looking than Heather. Trust me. I know. So kid, what'll you have? Beer?"

Toby shook her head in disgust. "Yeah, give me a High Test."

Sal pulled out a cold bottle of Extra Old Stock, popped the cap and set it down on a bar napkin. "Running a tab tonight?"

"Please."

Sal nodded. With a red pen, she wrote Toby's name and the price on a bar cheque, popped it into a glass tumbler by the cash register, then turned to the next customer in line.

Clutching her beer, Toby casually made her way to the back, past the murmur of women talking and laughing, the clinking of ice cubes against glass. An alternating red and blue flashing light glared uncomfortably. A woman in the aisle smoked an Indonesian cigarette, the scent of cloves distinct in the air. Toby liked to arrive at the club early and start with a couple games of pool. Later, she'd watch women dance, stroll around the room, flirt and, if her luck was high, ask someone home with her. Toby's need for intimacy lived close to the surface. She was always falling temporarily in love. Sal teased her mercilessly, calling her an official member in good standing of the Girlfriend of the Month Club.

At the back of the bar, Toby glanced at the chalk board where women signed their names for a turn at the pool table. The list was long and Toby didn't feel like waiting. She wandered to the edge of the dance floor. The heavy bass beat reverberated through her. She surveyed the women dancing. Couples bumping and grinding. Others on their first date, showing off, trying to look their most sexy, cool, femme, butch, intelligent or distinguished selves. Toby waved hello to Doris, the waitress, a sweet older femme, one of Sal's crowd from the old days, in the life since the early sixties. Doris wore tight black jeans and a red tank top. Toby could see a hint of black lace underneath. Long, silver earrings dangled from both ears. Her short, styled hair was reddish brown. While Sal watched out for the girls, Doris flirted and teased, like an older sister or aunt. Everyone knew not to take her flirtations seriously. She and Sammy had been together over fifteen years, no one knew exactly how long. Even Doris had to count it on her fingers.

"How's the action tonight Toby?" Doris supported a round cocktail tray on her right palm, above her shoulder. Folded bills were wedged between her fingers.

Toby sighed. "Same old people, same old faces." She took a swig of beer. "Am I just getting old?"

Doris frowned and studied Toby. "Oh pul-ease, sweetheart. How old are you? Twenty-three? Twenty-four?" Her left hand jumped instinctively to her hip.

"Twenty-six."

"Oh my god! Ready for the old folks home." Doris leaned in, kissed Toby's cheek and sighed. Some things never change she thought, twenty-six and already feeling over the hill. No wonder women my age rarely set foot in Rosie's. She shook her head sadly and turned on her heels to check on a group of baseball dykes crowded against the far wall.

Toby leaned on the brass railing surrounding the dance floor. The feel of cold metal under her fingers was comforting. Her eyes were drawn to a woman dancing alone in the far corner. Shaved head and earrings everywhere, in both ears, one eyebrow, lip. She wore black tights, a low cut top and a yellow and black leopard-spot mini skirt. Both arms were plastered with tattoos. With her eyes closed, she danced provocatively. Her hips moved in a rhythm from within. Most women looked around when they danced, aware of being watched. This woman seemed not to care. There was a mysterious, explosive energy about her. Palpable. Toby watched unabashedly.

Sherry Markowitz, a.k.a. Sher, a.k.a. SM, a.k.a. Sherry Mayhem, was ripped to the tits on some great Ecstasy scored from Kevin, the drummer in Guerrilla Punk, her band. She hadn't been to Rosie's in six months. She hated the place. It was depressing. In a fucking basement. No windows, seventies style disco lights, shitty outdated music, birkenstock girls talking politics, always some butch in a flannel shirt wanting her to donate money or sign some goddamned petition, as if she gave a fuck. Baseball nerds who actually went to the club in shorts and knee socks, suburban gay gals in pressed pleated pants two-stepping with their professional wives.

The only chicks who interested Sher were big bad butches with studded belts and leather jackets. Wild girls. Tough, proud girls who could fuck her all night long and all morning too. Girls who'd start a scene with her in public, end it somewhere private and continue for days. Girls with stamina. Girls who were mistaken for boys. Girls who weren't afraid of her desire, who liked her in black lace as much as they liked her in Doc Martens and oversized overalls. Girls who could satisfy her, rough in the sack, but gentle of heart. There were never enough girls like that. All she needed was one. Yet every time she found the perfect butch, it would last six months, maybe a year, and then she'd be so fucking bored that one day she'd snap and tell her girlfriend to get lost. Forever. Then she'd have to go back to the fucking dyke dump and search for another.

Toby stared at Sher, admiring how she moved. This was her kind of woman. Hot shit femme crazy bitch. She could tell by the way Sher danced — uninhibited, free, tuned to the rhythms of the music. By how she dressed. How she held her head high keeping one hand on her hip, thrusting her pelvis in a circular feminine sensuality, naked and brash. Toby loved the excitement, the drama of chasing someone new, and she especially liked to pursue wild women. She had an unfortunate weakness for bitchy femmes, prima donnas who would chew her up and spit her out, women who were absolutely arrogant, who thought everyone else owed them a fucking living. Toby craved women like that. And no matter how many lumps she took, she always went back for more.

She polished off her beer and set it down, waiting to

make her move, drinking in the bump and grind of Sher's sensuality, alert to the chaotic energy she thrust onto the dance floor with her angry grin, arrogant prance and deep dark eyes smouldering on a low flame.

Doris waltzed by Toby snatching her empty bottle.

"Another beer old lady?" she teased.

"Doris," she signalled with a nod of her head at the dance floor, "what's she drinking?"

Doris gave a quizzical look. "Who?"

"Over there. With the shaved head and all the earrings."

"Oh." She grinned. "Vodka martinis."

"Hmm." Toby was intrigued. There was something mysterious and sophisticated about a woman who drank martinis. Images of Hollywood, Greta Garbo, swanky New York nightclubs and Beverly Hills. It wasn't just a drink, it was a cocktail. Elegant and crisp, fascinating and dangerous. "Ever see her in here before?"

Doris inspected the woman again and nodded slowly. "Yeah. She's been here, but I haven't seen her in a long time. Last time, her hair was long and jet black. Before that it was platinum blonde like Madonna's, only wavy."

"Yeah?"

"I think she was with what's-her-name, but they broke up."

"Who?"

"I don't know her name. You know. Short, with cropped hair, leather jacket, jeans, drinks too much beer."

"Oh gee thanks. That really narrows it down." Toby glanced around the room. At least eighty women fit the description.

"Hey I'm a waitress, not a detective. Why don't you ask her to dance or something?"

"I'm getting there. Listen, bring me a martini. No, make that two."

"Whatever you say sweetie." Doris smiled and moved to the next table.

The DJ threw on an old Grace Slick song. The Ecstasy coursed through Sher's system. Her skin was open to everything, music pulsed through her, taking over. She moved effortlessly, aware of every bass note, every drum beat, every lead guitar lick. She was one with the music. The drugs blurred all boundaries, masked all outside distractions. She heard her heart beat, felt her blood pump. Focused inward, her skin vibrated in time with the music. The magic of its power excited her. She hadn't felt at home in her body for a long time. Waves of music pulsated melody down to her cunt, wet with frustrated desire. She hadn't had sex with anybody since Mo dumped her a month earlier. She was ready to kill if she didn't get some soon.

Sher stopped dancing and glanced around. Sweat poured down the sides of her face, soaked the space between her breasts. One hand on her hip, she scanned the crowd until her eyes settled on Toby, staring at her. Sher didn't like chicks checking her out without her permission. She strode over to where Toby stood, just as Doris returned with two martinis in long-stemmed glasses, straight up, with a twist — exactly how Sher had ordered her first one.

"Do I know you?" she asked.

"Can I buy you a drink?" Toby answered.

Sher laughed. "That's how you answer a question? With another question?"

Toby reached onto Doris' tray and removed the martinis. She held one out in front of her. "It's a martini. Would you like it?"

"There you go again. Another question."

"I bought it for you."

Doris cracked her gum and looked bored. "That's eight-fifty all together."

Toby smiled in Doris' direction. "I'm running a tab."

"Sure thing sweetie." She turned and carried on.

"Please," Toby persisted. "I really want you to have it."

"I bet you do."

"Come on. Take it." She felt ridiculous with her hand outstretched holding the drink in front of her. "It's for you."

"First answer my question." Sher put her other hand on her hip.

"Which one?"

"Boy, are you a work of art. My first question: Do I know you?"

"Oh. No. But I'd like you to."

Sher laughed, snatched the drink, swished past and ceremoniously plunked herself onto a high stool against the wall, crossing one leg over the other. Toby followed, hopping onto the seat beside.

Sher took a long sip of her martini. She put two fingers into her drink and smoothed cool liquid onto her forehead, still dripping with sweat. "So? Why do you want to know me?"

Toby shrugged nonchalantly. "I like how you look. And I like how you move."

Sher drank some more. "How do you know I don't have a girlfriend here tonight? A big butch who'd take you outside and smash her fists right through your skull just for talking to me?"

"If you have a girlfriend, how come she's letting a hot babe like you dance all by yourself?"

Sher began to swing one leg back and forth while she studied Toby. "You look familiar."

Toby shrugged.

"Did I meet you somewhere before?"

Toby frowned. "Doubt it. I'd remember if we'd met."

"What's your name?"

"Toby. What's yours?"

"What's your last name?"

"Lapinsky. What's your name?"

"Where you from?"

Toby tasted her martini. "Here."

"Here? You kidding?"

"No. I was born here."

"Really?"

"Yeah."

"I didn't think any Hebes were actually born in Vancouver. I thought we were all imports."

Toby winced at the word "Hebe" but didn't say anything. "My father hates winter. My parents moved here from Montreal before I was born. Aren't you going to tell me your name?"

Sher shrugged. "Why not? It's Sher."

"Cher? As in Sonny and...?"

"No stupid. With an 'S'. It's short for Sherry."

"Oh."

Sher raised her glass to her lips, knocked back the rest of her drink, set the empty glass down hard on the counter and whispered in Toby's ear, "Why don't you cut with the questions and ask me to dance, tough-girl?"

Toby placed her glass beside Sher's, jumped down from her stool and held out her hand. Madonna's *Justify My Love*, one of Sher's favourite songs, began. Alcohol slid through her system, warming, intoxicating her already drugged body. On the dance floor Sher was happy and safe. It was her domain. She could do anything: impress her admirers, antagonize her exes, make girlfriends jealous and pick up any woman she wanted. She knew Toby was hers from the moment their eyes met. Toby wasn't quite so sure. Sometimes women like Sher only wanted to lead her on, feed their egos, and at the end of the night, leave her alone with hopes high, desire roused. She saw a glint in Sher's eyes as they talked, but you could never be sure until you were sure. They lingered on the dance floor close to an hour, seducing each other, showing off, moving in and then back out again. Sweat poured from both women. They were oblivious to everyone else.

Sher moved forward. Excruciatingly slowly, she brought her lips to Toby's and they kissed. Softly at first, then passionately, dramatically, with a hint almost, of violence, as if each needed to wrench danger from the depths of the other. Toby felt her stomach flip as she clutched Sher tightly to her. They groped and kissed their way through three more songs.

"Let's go," Toby said. She knew the moment had arrived. She had Sher right where she wanted her. Without waiting for an answer, she gripped Sher's hand and led her off the dance floor toward the front door.

"Night Sal," she waved as they drifted past the bar to wait in the coat room line up.

"You girls play safe now," Sal said, giving Toby an "are you sure you know what you're doing?" look. Toby said nothing, and gave Sal a thumbs up signifying she knew what she was doing, even though, really, she didn't.

"I'll need my spare helmet," Toby said to Liz at the checkroom. Toby kept an extra one at the bar for these occasions.

"Sure thing." Liz bent down and handed over a beat up old red helmet. Then she retrieved Toby's newer black helmet and both women's jackets. Toby passed the red helmet to Sher, who examined her with a new level of interest.

"You didn't tell me we were riding in style," she said. Nothing turned Sher on more than being picked up by a handsome butch and taken home on the back of a motorcycle.

They didn't exactly behave like U Haul dykes — moving in together by their second date — however, after that first night, Sher and Toby were definitely an item. They spent every weekend together and most nights during the week. For a while, it lasted.

Six months into their relationship, they started to fight. Over the most stupid things. Sher was crabbier than usual, was often late or didn't show up at all. A few times she rejected Toby's advances when Toby wanted to make love. It was confusing. Sometimes Toby wanted to be with Sher. Other times she longed to be single again, so she could hang out at Rosie's, play pool and girl-watch. She didn't know what to do. Then one day she walked into her apartment after work and found a note.

Sher was bored enough to explode. She craved passion like an addict, needed to be free to do whatever the fuck she wanted without checking with someone first. She wanted to break up with Toby, but didn't know how. Toby was so goddamned nice, she felt like a bitch. She didn't want any hassles. Just out. Then Kevin called with good news. Guerrilla Punk would be hitting the road. Eddie Demon, bass player and manager, booked the band into a club in Toronto but first there were gigs in Calgary, Saskatoon, Winnipeg and Thunder Bay. They'd drive across the country in Eddie's old yellow school bus. Finally the band was going places.

Sher was thrilled. This was her big break. The morning they were leaving, she stopped at Toby's apartment and slipped a letter under the door.

The day Sher left, Toby hopped on her bike and rode. Across the Lion's Gate Bridge to the North Shore and up the winding Squamish highway. The rain stopped for the first time in thirty-three days. Just when people all over town were reinventing Noah and the Ark jokes, waging bets on whether or not the wet weather would continue for forty days and forty nights, the sun came out. Bright green leaves dripped and dried on both sides of the highway. The blue burst so bright it hurt Toby's eyes. She opened the throttle full out and careened expertly up the mountain highway. Everything was so beautiful she couldn't stay depressed. No matter how hard she tried. At a roadside stand, Toby sat on a damp picnic bench and ate fish and chips. Above, on a telephone wire, two robins argued, one harassing the other, chasing it from one spot to the next. When she'd had enough bird watching, she zipped into town, weaving wildly in and out of cars, until she parked in front of Rosie's.

Sal smiled from behind the bar then eyed Toby questioningly. It was the first time she'd seen Toby without Sher since they got together. Trouble in paradise.

"Hey Toby. What can I get you hon?"

Toby leaned her elbows on the counter. "A new girl-friend?"

Sal nodded knowingly. "I thought something was up. Here," she filled a mug from the draft tap. "Have a beer on me." She plunked the draft onto a paper coaster and leaned on the counter with both hands. "So? What happened kid?"

Toby hoisted her beer and took a long swallow. "Same old story Sal. It's over. Finished."

Sal studied Toby's face. "No offense or anything Tobe. But you don't look all that broken up about it."

Toby lifted her mug for a long swallow. "I know. It's weird Sal. Usually right about now, when a girl leaves me, I feel depressed. But this time — I don't know, I feel...relieved."

Sal thought about it for a moment. "That's okay. Feelings don't have to make sense. Anyway, I've missed you."

"Yeah?"

"Sure kid. Nobody here can play a decent game of pool. Nobody else can give me a run for my money the way you can."

Toby grinned.

Sal strode to the end of the bar and over to the other side, where she placed her arm around Toby's shoulder. "Hey Doris! Cover for me behind the bar will ya honey?"

"Sure thing Sal. Let me just grab these mugs."

"Come on. Let's play a game right now. I want to see if you still got it."

"Still got it!? Hey! Remember who you're talking to here Sal. Course I still got it."

"Course you do kid." Sal turned and headed toward the pool table.

Toby scooped up her mug and followed Sal to familiar turf at the back of the bar.

▼▼▼

Canadian Shmadian

▼ It is Kayla Rosenbaum's first act of rebellion. She is six years old, in grade one. It is the first day of school. The children are sitting at freshly varnished wooden desks, carefully arranged in neat rows, when the teacher tells them to stand. Kayla pushes back her chair. It scrapes the floor, making a loud, high-pitched sound. The girl beside her giggles. Kayla giggles back and nervously covers her mouth with her hand. At the front of the class hangs a huge picture of Queen Elizabeth, diamond studded crown in her hair, string of white pearls around her neck, hands folded politely in her lap.

"We will now sing God Save the Queen," the young teacher announces, eyes bright, voice cheerful.

Kayla feels fire in her belly, every fibre of her being screaming not to sing. The day before she had sat on Zayde Avram's knee.

"Chava," he said to her, for he never called her by her English name, Kayla, only by her Jewish name. "Don't ever forget who you are. Some people vill tell you to ect like a Canadian because you vere born here, but it doesn't matter. You vill always be a Jew, no matter vat country you live in. Don't ever forget dat."

Kayla was fidgeting with the buttons on his sweater, the

brown one he always wore in winter. She didn't understand what he was trying to tell her, but she heard every word.

"You'd never believe some of the tings I've seen," Zayde said. "In 1942 — maybe it vas '43 or '44 — can't remember exactly. In any case, it vas deh first time in five years I took a day off. So, I took your bubbe, your father and your Aunt Rosa to deh lake. Do you know vat I saw dere?"

Kayla shook her head.

"A beeg sign. Everybody could see it. Do you know vat it said?"

She shook her head again.

"It said 'No dogs or Jews allowed.'" Zayde looked deep into Kayla's eyes. "You understand Chava?"

She pictured herself, half dog, half child, down on her hands and knees with a collar and leash around her neck.

"Farshteis?"

Kayla nodded yes. She understood. Deep in her soul.

Today, on the first day of school, Zayde Avram's words repeat in her brain. She looks around the room. All the other children are singing the song.

God save our gracious queen. God save our noble queen. God save the queen.

They all know the words. How come they know the song and she doesn't? To Kayla, god is a word you hear in the synagogue, all dressed up on Saturday morning. The rabbi in his black robe, yarmulke on his head, tallis around his neck begins a prayer,

Shema Yisrael adonai eloheinu adonai echad.

Hear oh Israel the Lord our God, the Lord is one.

Hundreds of voices all around the shul repeat after him, singing loudly and softly, off-key and melodically, the ancient prayer. Kayla never imagined she'd hear about God from her teacher at school.

What does God have to do with a queen? Who is the queen and how come Kayla's never heard of her before? Is she like the queen in *Sleeping Beauty*? Mean and powerful? Is her teacher afraid of the queen? Should she be? Kayla looks up at the queen's picture. She doesn't look very nice. She's not even smiling. Kayla stares at the mouth of the girl beside her. If she watches closely, maybe she can figure out the words and sing too. Zayde's voice floods her head. "Don't ever forget who you are."

Her heart pounds. She sees herself as a dog on a leash. The queen scowls down, but Kayla has her zayde to think about. So, she sits back in her chair and waits. Her strange behaviour does not escape the teacher's attention. She safety pins a note for Kayla's mother to the back of her shirt. The first day of school and Kayla is in trouble already.

Esther Rosenbaum plops a raw meatball into a frying pan filled with Crisco. It sizzles. On another burner rests a big pot of water for spaghetti. On the counter she has laid out two cans of tomato sauce, an onion, some mushrooms. The air in the kitchen is warm, thick with fried grease. Sweat drips down the back of Esther's neck and from under her breasts. She is still in her work clothes, a cotton print, knee-length dress, a new outfit purchased wholesale on her employee's discount at K Mart, where she is a clerk in the ladies wear department. When the meatballs are cooked, Esther plans to ease her full figure out of her snug lycra panty girdle and into a loose fitting house dress. She is tired and sore from standing all afternoon. Petula Clark sings *Downtown* from a small portable radio on the counter, a present from her sister Gloria. Esther hums along. As she drops the last meatball into hot oil, the front door bursts open. She hears her husband's heavy footsteps, followed by her daughter's laughter. They clamour into the kitchen.

"Esther I'm home," Morris shouts.

"I can see that." She doesn't turn from the stove.

"Our daughter has a note. Pinned on her back. Did you see?"

"What?" Esther lays her grease-covered spatula down on the counter and turns around. Kayla shrinks back against her father's leg.

When Esther reads the note she says, "So? You'll sing the song. What's so terrible?"

"Esther! How can you say that?" Morris disagrees. "Why should we save the queen? What has the queen ever done for us? Huh? Did she stop the holocaust? Did she open the doors to this country when she could have saved hundreds of thousands of Jews? What about your Uncle Yitzchak and his family? Or all my aunts and uncles who died in the camps? What's the queen got to say about that Esther!?"

"Morris, calm down. You'll have a heart attack and then where will we be? The teacher wants her to sing — she'll sing." A waft of grey smoke rises from the frying pan. The faint smell of burning meat permeates the kitchen. Esther spins dramatically back to the stove. "My food is burning! Everybody out of the kitchen!" She lowers the heat and flips the well done meatballs. Hot oil splashes her forearm. "Ow!" Morris and Kayla glance at each other guiltily and slink out of the room.

After dinner, Kayla sits on the living room couch next to Zayde Avram while he reads the Yiddish newspaper. He holds it up high with both hands, nodding or shaking his head every so often. Sometimes he makes a clicking sound with his tongue against his teeth. Kayla tries to make the sound too. It tickles the tip of her tongue. Zayde flips the page and folds the paper along the middle. Kayla looks up at the print, head tilted. She can't read yet, but she recognizes the Hebrew characters. They are the same letters she sees in the prayer book at shul. There are no pictures in the Yiddish paper like there is in the English one her dad reads. Only Hebrew letters, black on white across the page. Zayde hums softly under his breath as he reads. Kayla stares at his face. He has grey, black stubble all over his chin and cheeks. He reaches up and scratches his neck. Kayla's mind wanders. The tune of the god save our queen song fills her head. She remembers she wants to ask Zayde about it.

"Zayde?" she tugs at the wool sleeve of his sweater. "Do you know the queen?"

"Who?"

"The queen. We got her picture in the front of my class."

"Oh. Deh queen." He folds his paper neatly in half and sets it down in his lap. "Deh queen," he repeats, nodding his head. He removes the red pack from his shirt pocket, takes out a cigarette, puts the brown end between his lips, reaches in his pants pocket for his silver lighter, lights his cigarette and snaps the lighter shut. Kayla watches curls of grey blue smoke rise to the ceiling, filling the living room.

"Deh queen." He says again, shaking his head. "Vhere vould I meet deh queen Chava? Lately, I haven't seen her on our block."

Kayla pictures the queen on her street. It makes her giggle. In her fancy long dress and crown, walking past their house, or in a carriage with horses, like the prince in *Cinderella*. "I have to sing a song about the queen at school," she tells Zayde, "and it has God in it too."

He looks down at her and crinkles up his forehead like he does when he's mad at something on the news. "Vhy should you sing to deh queen? Dat's crazy. Who told you to sing such a song?"

Kayla feels like she is going to cry. She stares at her feet and nervously clicks together the brand new black patent leather shoes her dad brought home from the shoe store he manages. The leather is stiff and she has blisters on the back of both ankles. "My mom," she says.

"Oh." He nods his head slowly and puffs on his cigarette. "Vhy didn't you say so? Dat's a different story." Kayla sneaks a look at him. He holds one hand out in front, like he's about to catch a ball. "Sure. Your mother knows vat she's talking about. Efter all, she finished high school. Am I right?"

Kayla nods.

"Sure. You should always listen to your mother, Chava. She's a smart voman. It's important to do vell in school. Isn't dat vat I always tell you?"

She nods again.

"But, you don't have to sing such songs at home. Vat ve do here — dat's a different story. Farshteis?"

"Yes Zayde."

He kisses the top of her head and shakes his finger at her. "Oy Chava, you're getting so beeg, I can hardly recognize you. Now, all of deh sudden you've got problems at school. And you're so young still. Such mishegus I never heard." He shakes his head, picks up his paper, and resumes clicking his tongue and reading.

Kayla sits quietly beside Zayde for a while and thinks. Grade one is going to be a lot harder than she imagined. There's so much to remember. Which desk is hers, not to speak unless the teacher calls on her, names of kids she's never met before, how to walk to school without getting lost, all the letters of the alphabet and all the numbers too. The whole thing is very tiring. She leans against Zayde's arm, closes her eyes and listens to his melodic voice begin to sing the sad sweet sounds of an old Yiddish lullaby:

Offin pripachuck brent ah fire-al
Un in shtib iz heys
Un da Rebbe learnet kleynah kinderlach
Dem aleph beys
On the little hearth, a fire is burning bright
The school is so warm
The old teacher's telling all the children there
How the alphabet was born.

Zayde Avram has another name. Kayla has heard the man from her dad's work call him Abe. Some people call him Abraham. Everyone in her family has a lot of names. Even her. Zayde Avram and Bubbe Sophie call her Chava. Her dad calls her Kayla and last year, when she started kindergarten, her mom said everyone had to call her Kay.

"The other kids'll tease her Morris," Esther had argued, as the family rode out to the country for a Sunday drive in the beat-up red station wagon. Kayla sat in front between her parents. Her baby sister Raizel lay in her mother's lap sleeping. Bubbe and Zayde sat in the back seat. Her older brother Herschel was all the way in the back, lying down, his feet up on the ceiling.

"So? What about Herschel? Didn't we send him to school with his real name?"

"That's different. He's a boy. Oh look!" Esther pointed to a farmer's vegetable stand by the side of the road. A hand drawn sign advertised ten ears of corn for twenty-five cents. Dust rose from the dirt road as Morris sped past.

"We named our daughter after Pa's sister, may she rest

in peace. Her name was Chava. Didn't we change it enough already when we called her Kayla?"

"I've made my decision Moe."

"Stop it Esther. My name is Morris. It was Morris when you met me and it'll be Morris till the day I die. I'm warning you. You're making me crazy with this name thing."

"There's another one! Twelve for twenty-five cents. Even better. Morris stop the car!"

"Huh?"

"Fresh corn. Look."

Morris stepped on the brake and veered to the right. They bumped and rumbled over stones and potholes, stopping at the side of the gravel road.

Kayla is seven years old. The school caretaker lowers the red ensign from the flag pole and replaces it with a shiny new flag, the red and white maple leaf. The picture of the queen stays up in the front of the classroom, but something has changed. Kayla's teacher loves the new flag. She beams when she says Canada is a real country now. We are truly Canadian.

"Canadian Shmadian," Zayde says when Kayla tells him. "Don't you tink deh Jews in Germany tought dey vere good Germans? A flag doesn't make any difference at all for us Chava."

She tries to make sense of it. Her teacher thinks the flag makes a big difference, but Zayde doesn't. She figures it's just like singing the god save our queen song, something she has to do in school but not at home. She decides she will be proud of the new maple leaf flag in the day, but at night she won't speak or even think about it. One evening at supper she makes a mistake.

"What did you do in school today?" her father asks, biting into a chicken leg.

"We did arts and crafts," Kayla says proudly. "Everyone had to cut and paste our own flags, maple leaf ones, and we're going to hang them on the walls of our class." Too late she realizes what she has said. She looks over to Zayde to see if he is angry but it doesn't seem like he even heard. He's hunched over his plate, shovelling spoonfuls of chicken soup into his mouth. A small string of soggy celery clings to his chin. Kayla looks around to see if anyone else has noticed. Her father is tearing the last bits of meat from a chicken leg, Bubbe is spooning boiled potatoes onto Zayde's plate, her mother is chomping on a chicken wing with one hand and stuffing mushed-up carrots into Raizel's mouth with the other. Herschel looks up and sticks his tongue out, revealing chewed up corn and peas.

1967. Kayla is nine. Every day the teacher wants her to learn a new song. They still sing *God Save the Queen* at the start of each day, but now they have to learn another one.

Oh Canada, our home and native land.

Zayde Avram says their land is the land of Israel. He says it belongs to the Jews and they finally got it back after thousands of years.

"A little late, but, at least, God villing, ve have a place to go now," he tells Kayla and Herschel.

It is spring. Zayde sits on a red plastic lawn chair on the front porch, a cigarette dangles from his lips, a glass of seltzer water in hand. Herschel bounces a red, white and blue rubber ball against the aluminum garage door. Each time it hits a thunderous, hollow boom blasts into the street and the door rattles violently. Kayla stops skipping rope.

"Why is it late?" she asks.

Herschel rolls his eyes. "Why do you think stupid?" He catches the ball as it bounces back to him.

"I'm not stupid. Am I Zayde?" She wanders over to Zayde Avram and leans against his leg.

"Shah. Shah. Vat's deh use in fighting? Dat's how vars start. Do you understand vat a var is?"

Herschel says he does. Kayla doesn't really know, but the word sounds scary. It feels funny in her stomach to hear Zayde say it. Like she knows what it means even though she doesn't.

"If ve'd had deh state of Israel during deh var, Jews by deh tousands, by deh hundreds of tousands vould've been saved. It vould've been a whole different story. Who knows? Maybe my brothers Shlomo and Feivel vould've lived, not to mention my little sister Chavala. Dats who you're named after," he reminds Kayla. "And Herman — oy my young brother, Herman." He crushes his cigarette in a small aluminum ashtray on the armrest. Kayla watches as Zayde sucks in his bottom lip and rubs the worry lines on his forehead. Something bad happened to her great Uncle Herman. When Zayde was a young man, Herman drowned in a river.

The next day in school, the teacher recites the words to the new "Oh Canada" song. Kayla puts up her hand.

"My land is the land of Israel," she proclaims. The children laugh.

"Yes, but you were born in Canada," the teacher says.

Kayla's face burns red. She wishes she could disappear. All the kids are giggling, staring at her.

"So this is your land," the teacher insists.

Kayla frowns. "My zayde...I mean my grandfather says the land of Israel is my land." The kids all laugh again.

"Well," the teacher admits, "that's true. The Hebrew

people say they lived in the area that is now called Israel thousands of years ago. But Canada is the country you were born in, the country we all live in. So this is your native land."

The teacher is making Kayla angry, but she knows you can't argue with grown-ups, especially when they have their minds made up. She decides to try and learn the song.

When Kayla finally can remember it, they have to learn a whole new song.

Ca-na-da. Now we are twenty million. Ca-na-da...It's our hundredth anniversary of con-fed-er-a-tion...Church bells will ring, ring, ring.

Like a good pupil, Kayla learns the words, but they feel awkward in her mouth. Something is still wrong. These aren't her songs. They sound like Christmas carols.

Silent night, holy night.

Fa-la-la-la-la-la-la-la-la.

Every December she has to sing the strange melodies, the unfamiliar words. Most of the time, she does as she is told. But every so often, something inside snaps and she rebels. She stares down at her desk, refusing to sing. Her songs are in Hebrew, not English. Zayde Avram would not want her to sing.

At ten school suddenly grows worse. Her new teacher, Mrs. Beachum, is mean. She is much older than any teacher Kayla has ever had, older even than Zayde Avram. Her grey hair is curled. Mrs. Beachum wears navy blue or grey woollen dresses, with a flower-shaped silver broach pinned on one side. Her voice is creepy, high-pitched. The skin on her arms is loose and shaky. She never smiles or laughs. She has thick lines on her forehead and two deep grooves just above her nose that go down in a v shape. She makes the kids sit quietly with their hands folded in front of them, all the time. When they want to say something, they must raise their hands and wait. When she calls on them, they have to stand beside their desks before they speak. When they're bad or don't know the answer, she hauls them up to the front of the class and forces them to hold out their hands, palms up. Then, in front of everyone, she smacks them ten times on each hand with a yardstick. If they don't cry, she gets really mad and beats them more. Behind her back, the children call her Mrs. Beat Them.

From her seat in the third row, Kayla can clearly see Mrs. Beat Them's yardstick in its place, leaning up against the chalk board in the corner, by the pencil sharpener. It's almost as tall as Kayla. It has numbers written all up and down, with little black lines between the numbers. Sometimes late in the afternoon when Kayla is tired she sees a face on the yardstick. The numbers blur together and the yardstick grows eyes, mean eyes just like Mrs. Beat Them's. The top end of the stick sways and swaggers, like tree monsters who grow faces and arms after dark.

By the second month of school Kayla knows her teacher hates some kids more than others. She hates Kathy Fielding, who has only two different dresses and isn't very good at spelling. Kathy is constantly hauled up to the front of the class for wrong answers. Mrs. Beat Them hates Harry Hashimoto. She says during the war his people were enemies of Canada. Harry keeps his mouth quiet and his head down. Never raises his hand to answer questions. Mrs. Beat Them hates Charlie Spearchief and Donald Jones, two boys who live on Kayla's street. Some kids say it's because they're always late and get into fights, but Kayla thinks her teacher hates everybody who isn't white. Mrs. Beat Them hates Marty Leibowitz. Marty is smart and always gets the answers right, even when he hasn't been paying attention. Mrs. Beat Them says all Jews are rich and it's their own fault everybody hates them because they don't believe in Christ. She hates Kayla Rosenbaum even more than she hates Marty Liebowitz, because Kayla isn't rich and that wrecks Mrs. Beat Them's theory.

Kayla doesn't like school anymore. She even faked a cold so she could stay home for two days. She hasn't told her parents yet about Mrs. Beat Them. They're grown-ups and she thinks they won't believe her. That she's just saying so to stay home from school. Kayla hasn't had the yardstick, but worries about it constantly.

Every morning they sing *God Save The Queen, Oh Canada*, and *Jesus Loves Me This I Know*. Kayla has never had to sing Jesus before, but the words were easy, so she just does it. Mrs. Beat Them has started a new thing called Bible studies. Every Friday she teaches about Jesus and all these other people, like Mary and the Holy Ghost. Kayla knows Zayde Avram would be mad if he knew she was learning Jesus stuff, but she can't see any way out of it, so she hasn't told him yet. She just pretends it's like spelling or arithmetic, another thing she has to read about and memorize.

It's December and Mrs. Beat Them is in a better mood. Her son-in-law brought a big green Christmas tree into the classroom. It sits in the corner at the front, beside the pencil sharpener, where the yardstick used to be. When the tree arrived, Mrs. Beat Them moved the stick to the other corner behind her desk. The tree is so tall it touches the ceiling. Pine needles prick Kayla's arm whenever she walks by. It smells fresh, like the lawn in summer. Little broken bits fall to the ground and leave a trail down the seat aisles. Sometimes they get inside Kayla's shoes and make her feet itchy. Kayla and her classmates spend a lot of time on arts and crafts, making ornaments for the tree. First they string popcorn onto long strands of black thread, using a needle to push through the middle of each piece of popcorn. Kayla likes the way it feels when she pushes the point through the soft kernels, but sometimes her hand slips and the needle pricks her finger. Whenever Mrs. Beat Them turns her back, the kids shove popcorn into their mouths.

Another day Mrs. Beat Them says to take out their scissors and pencil crayons. They are going to make decorations for the tree and the walls of the room with construction paper. Mrs. Beat Them passes out plastic stencils for the children to trace. There are reindeer, snowflakes, angels, five pointed stars and candy canes. Mrs. Beat Them allows the children to put their decorations onto the tree. It is the first time Kayla remembers her teacher being nice.

During December they spend a lot of time singing Christmas carols. Mrs. Beat Them knows lots Kayla has never heard before. She looks around. All the other kids, except Marty, seem to know them. Kayla is scared to admit she doesn't know the words. Her teacher will be angry. So she opens and closes her mouth and pretends. It works for a while. Then, without warning, Mrs. Beat Them is heading down her row, cold grey eyes fixed on Kayla. She continues opening and closing her mouth, as her knees start to shake under her desk and her heart starts to pound in her chest. Mrs. Beat Them looms over Kayla. Everyone stops singing. There is silence in the room.

"Well, Miss Rosenbaum. Is there some reason why you are not singing with the rest of the class?"

Kayla doesn't know what to say. If she tells the truth she'll get in trouble for not knowing the songs. If she lies she'll get in trouble too. She feels a quivering in her stomach, a sour taste in her mouth. Mrs. Beat Them looks taller than usual. Kayla shrugs and flinches, waiting.

"Is that how proper young ladies answer a teacher's question?" she booms.

Kayla thinks hard. She is so frightened, she can't remember the answer. She sucks in her lower lip.

Mrs. Beat Them chuckles meanly and surveys the room. "Maybe someone else can tell us how proper young ladies should answer teacher's question?"

Cindy Johnson, miss goody-two-shoes, leaps to her feet. "I know Mrs. Beachum."

"Yes."

"Proper young ladies stand when they are speaking to their teachers."

Oh. That. With her head down, Kayla grips the sides of her desk, pushes her chair back, scraping the floor with a loud screech and stands behind her desk. Her weak knees shake. She is having trouble breathing. Her chest is tight. She breathes quickly in and out of her open mouth.

"I think our little Hebrew friend needs to learn a lesson she won't forget," Mrs. Beat Them bellows.

Kayla peers behind her teacher and sees the yardstick in its special corner. She sees its mean face. It is laughing at her, practically rubbing its hands in anticipation. She considers bolting for the door. Racing all the way home and telling Zayde. He'd save her. They'd fly together to the land of Israel. It would be hot and sunny, just like Zayde says and they'd be safe and far away from Mrs. Beat Them, her Christmas carols and her yardstick. Before Kayla has the chance to do anything, the teacher reaches out, grips her arm and hauls her to the front of the class. Kayla sees Marty Leibowitz as she passes. His dark brown eyes are proud and angry. He smiles a bit and nods.

In front of the whole class, Mrs. Beat Them forces Kayla to hold out her hands, palms up, while she goes to the corner to fetch her stick. Kayla's whole body is shaking. She looks up at her teacher's face, hoping for last minute mercy. But the eyes are cold, as usual. Mrs. Beat Them draws the yardstick high above her head and slams it down onto Kayla's right hand. The sound of the wood as it cracks against her skin is worse than the sting. There is a sharp blast of pain, then a tingling that spreads across Kayla's palm. Her eyes widen. Mrs. Beat Them raises the yardstick and strikes again at the same hand. Whack. The second slap hurts more. Up and down the stick flies. Over Mrs. Beat Them's head and down on Kayla's palm. All Kayla's senses focus. The sound echoes in her ears. Swoosh. Whack. Swoosh. Crack. Sharp, red, hot pain rips through Kayla's hand, travels up her arm. Seven, eight, nine, ten, Kayla counts silently but does not cry out.

A boiling rage, a fierce pride grips her. She concentrates, thinking about the look in Marty's eyes. About Zayde Avram, how he escaped from Russia when he was just seventeen. About her great uncles, Shlomo and Fievel and her aunt Chava, all killed in the war. About Uncle Herman who drowned trying to escape from Russia. About Harry Hashimoto, Kathy Fielding and Charlie Spearchief. With each crack of the stick, Kayla becomes more determined not to utter a sound. Mrs. Beat Them starts to work on Kayla's other hand. Lifts the stick high and slaps it down. Chin out, mouth set, Kayla stares at the shiny silver broach on Mrs. Beat Them's dress. Defiance burns in her heart. She concentrates. She is both here and not here. Lips clamped tight together, Kayla stuffs her voice down her throat and into her belly. Her spirit floats up, hovers just below the ceiling, watches her own body stand rigid. With each strike, Mrs.

Beat Them grows angrier. When she has beat Kayla ten times on each hand, she stops and studies Kayla's face. She sees bold disobedience. Steel, stone and rock. Mrs. Beat Them raises her arm and belts the child three more times on each hand, until the skin breaks and a small trickle of blood appears in her right palm.

Silently, Mrs. Beat Them replaces the yardstick in its corner. Her eyes shoot hate as she orders Kayla back to her seat. Kayla walks slowly down the aisle, head up, teeth clenched, eyes hard. She lowers herself onto her wooden chair, lays her throbbing hands out on the desk in front of her. Mrs. Beat Them continues with Christmas carols. Kayla does not even pretend to sing. From across the room, Harry Hashimoto flashes a conspiratorial look, points to Mrs. Beat Them and draws a finger across his throat. The air in the class room is hot. Hate surges in Kayla's chest. Her heart races as she replays the scene over and over in her mind. She wants to hit someone, wants to run away, wants to knock the Christmas tree to the floor, wants to scream. She is vaguely aware of her classmates singing, voices muted. She sits and waits for the bell to ring.

Kayla's hands burn as she walks home in the bitter cold. Her wool mittens scratch raw skin. She kicks a pop can hard, watches it ricochet into the side of a parked car, enjoys the sound as it clickety clacks back to the icy pavement. She holds her hands stiffly at her sides. Tears well up in her eyes. By the time she reaches home she is crying and doesn't try to hide it. She knocks on the door for someone to let her in. Bubbe Sophie is always home after school and the door never locked, but the thought of turning the knob with her aching hands is too much for Kayla to bear. She waits until Bubbe comes to the door.

Sophie opens it, surprised to see her granddaughter

standing there. "Chava. What's a matter? You forgot how to open a door?"

Kayla steps inside the front hall. Bubbe looks at her face.

"Mamelah. What's a matter? You're crying. Did somebody hurt you?"

Kayla flings herself into Bubbe's arms. Through sobs, she tells her everything. About Mrs. Beat Them, about getting the yardstick, about her teacher who hates kids and makes them all, even the two Jewish kids, sing *Jesus Loves Me This I Know* and make Christmas tree ornaments, and how she wanted to see Kayla cry but she wouldn't, not until she got home.

"I hate her and I hate school and I'm never going back," Kayla announces.

Bubbe helps her off with her mittens and coat and leads her to the bathroom, where she applies iodine to her hands. Bubbe blows to cool the stinging. Then she takes Kayla into the kitchen, makes hot chocolate and lets her eat as many cookies as she wants while they wait for Esther to come home from work. When she does, Bubbe tells her daughter-in-law the whole story.

"My poor baby," Esther says, holding Kayla. "Why didn't you tell us about this before?"

Kayla shrugs. She honestly doesn't know. It seems stupid that she didn't tell them. She sits quietly at the kitchen table beside Bubbe, who rubs her back and pushes curls of black hair out of her eyes. By the time Zayde and Morris come home, Esther is yelling and cursing.

"My god Esther," Morris says when he hears the news. "How could a woman do this to a child?" He examines Kayla's hands, bruised purple.

"Tomorrow morning Morris. Bright and early, we're going to the school to talk to the principal. Kay you can stay home for the next few days. Your bubbe will take care of you. I'm telling you Morris, I think we should call a lawyer. Maybe we should sue."

"Who can afford a lawyer Esther? We can barely make the mortgage payment this month."

"There's got to be something we can do. We can't let that monster get away with this. Look what she's done to our baby. Oy Kayla, I wish you had told us sooner about this — this teacher. Tell me Morris. How does someone like this become a teacher? It's not right."

Three days later Mrs. Beat Them opens her carol book to her favourite song, *Silent Night.* "Oh," she says, "all children of the Hebrew faith, please stand."

Kayla looks over at Marty nervously. He shrugs. They stand.

"Please leave the room and wait in the hall," Mrs. Beat Them orders. Under the silent stares of their classmates, Kayla and Marty walk to the front of the class, open the heavy wood door and step out to the hall. Mrs. Beat Them closes the door behind them.

The beige tile floor is cold, but Kayla and Marty sit down anyway. Kayla feels like she's about to burst into tears. Marty reaches in his pocket for a pencil and a small piece of paper.

"Hey. It's not so bad. Wanna play hangman?"

Kayla shrugs.

"Come on. It's better than staying in there."

"Yeah. I guess."

"You go first." He hands the paper and pencil to Kayla. She grasps them carefully, hands still tender from the yardstick. Sounding muffled, they hear the class singing *Silent Night.*

Marty doesn't show it to Kayla, but he's worried about recess. The other boys in his class hate him almost as much as Mrs. Beat Them does. They'll think he's lucky to be out in the hall instead of in class. Later, they'll take out their hate with their fists. While Kayla draws a hangman's noose and lays a series of dashes on the page, Marty counts on his fingers to figure out how many years he has to wait before he's old enough to quit school.

Kayla plays the game, but she, too, is thinking about the future. Thinking that when she grows up, she'll be a teacher, only she won't be like Mrs. Beat Them at all. She'll never hit kids. She'll never make some kids wait in the hall while the others stay inside. She thinks there must be a rule against it, but she knows her parents already talked to the principal, so maybe there isn't. She thinks about Zayde Avram and the Land of Israel and wishes she lived there. Maybe that's where she'll live when she grows up. Run away from Canada to the place where no one, not even a teacher, can make her sing Christmas songs or send her out in the hall. She looks over at Marty. Kayla is glad he's in her class. Without him, she'd be in this mess all alone. Just to be nice, she gives him an easy clue and he figures out her word. As she hands the pencil and paper to Marty, they hear their classmates singing the next song.

Peace on earth, goodwill to men...

▼ ▼ ▼

Women Who Make My Knees Weak

▼ Aunt Rose

The first femme in my life was my Auntie Rose. When I was a child she was young, beautiful, glamorous and a little crazy. One time, when Aunt Rose was first dating Uncle Marvin, she raced into our house and begged my mother to let her take me out for the day. She wanted to see what Marvin was like with children before she decided to marry him. My mother must have agreed because moments later I was sitting between them in the front seat of Marvin's 1957 Chevy convertible, my five year old legs stretched straight out in front of me. I looked from one to the other and then ahead, excited. I was out on a date with my aunt and her boyfriend.

Even at the age of five, I was a butch. As we drove, I studied Marvin. He sat behind the wheel with his legs spread wide, so I spread mine too. When Marvin would turn to talk to my aunt, he raised his eyebrows and smiled at her with one side of his mouth. Sometimes he'd slick back his hair with the palm of his right hand. I tried all his moves. My aunt laughed and ruffled my hair affectionately. The nails on her hands were long and painted red. Sitting close to her like that, I could smell her perfume. I turned to watch her as she crossed her legs, adjusted her skirt and looked over at Marvin. They were talking about grown-up things I couldn't understand so I sat quietly listening and watching. It was a warm spring day. Aunt Rose said she was hot and undid the top three buttons on her sweater. Marvin glanced over and stared at her open neck, his eyes wide. The car in front of us came to a sudden stop, but Marvin didn't see. I tugged on his shirt sleeve and pointed.

"Oh my god!" he blurted and slammed on the brakes. We were all thrown forward into the dashboard. My face slammed into the hard chrome knob on the radio. We came to a stop inches behind the other car. For a moment, we sat in stunned silence.

"Everyone okay?" Marvin asked, rubbing his shoulder.

"Oh my god!" Aunt Rose stared at me. "Marvin look what you've done!"

Blood spilled from somewhere, dripping onto my pants. I tasted something salty in my mouth and my lip was tingling. Aunt Rose fiddled in her purse and pulled out a white lace hanky to wipe my face.

"Bobby honey, does it hurt?"

I shook my head. I didn't feel anything and was enjoying the attention. As she leaned over, I could see right down her shirt. I tried to imagine what it was about seeing her breasts that caused Marvin to forget he was driving.

"Her lip is split wide open," Aunt Rose snarled at him. "We'll have to take her home now." My aunt pulled me onto her lap and, holding the hanky over my wound she nestled me against her bosom and held me there all the way home.

Cecile LaRoche
When I came out in the late seventies, butch and femme were politically incorrect. My first lover was a femme, but

after we broke up, I found her type scarce in the lesbian world. There was a small dyke bar called The Village under a strip joint in downtown Toronto, owned and run by an older butch named Jan. I was barely legal drinking age. At first Jan gave me a hard time because I looked so young, but after a while she got to know me and decided she liked me because I wasn't "one of those damn feminists."

"Always tellin' me what to think and what to wear," Jan would complain as she poured another pint of beer from the tap, ashes from her brown filtered cigarette floating down onto the counter. "Hah! Most of those broads are straight anyway or just came out yesterday. Think they can come into my place and act like they know the score. Where were they in the sixties or the fifties when I was gettin' my head busted up on Cherry Beach by the damn cops? I'll tell you where they were." She shook her head and blew smoke out the side of her mouth. "In grade school. Married to some guy. Havin' babies, and choosin' china patterns. Now here they are tellin' me I'm oppressin' them just because I know who I am and I know what I like. Damn feminists."

"Yeah," I agreed, though I was too young to know what else to say. In my heart I knew she was right. Jan never let "the feminists" know how she really felt. They represented most of her business. Opening the bar was the fulfilment of a long-held dream to run a club for her and her friends. A place that was theirs, where they were welcome.

"Do you know why I called this place The Village?" she asked me on a slow night.

I shrugged.

She laughed. "Course you don't Bobby. You're too damn young. It's after THE Village. You know. Greenwich Village in New York. First time I ever went to a gay bar was in The Village. Damn if I even remember what the place was called."

Jan was always trying to get her old friends — her butch pals and their femmes — to hang out at The Village, but they were outnumbered by the ever-growing population of over-all-covered lesbian feminists. In cruel irony, Jan's friends were pushed aside by the Birkenstock set. They didn't feel comfortable going to a club where at any moment some woman with long hair, khaki shorts and hairy legs might start thumping her fist on the table and accuse them of colluding with the patriarchy for wearing a tie, or make up and high heels. A few times a fight almost broke out when one of the butches was pushed past her limit. Most of the time, however, they simply felt unwelcome and stayed away.

"Ain't much different than gettin' yelled at in the streets," Jan would say, shaking her head sadly.

The Village didn't last long. By the end of the first year, the owner of the building figured out what kind of clientele the club was serving and refused to renew the lease. Jan didn't have the energy to fight or the heart to carry on. The bar closed down.

It was 1981. I was a butch looking for femmes in a sea of androgyny. There was only one thing to do. I took to falling for straight women. Cecile LaRoche was my first. I met her at a fag bar on Yonge Street, a small place that had been there for years. On weekends they had drag shows and a DJ. The rest of the time customers pumped quarters into the juke box. Tired old queens, pretty young men, working girls and all kinds of dykes drank beer, met with friends and searched for someone new. One Tuesday night I was sitting at the bar on a high stool when a woman in her mid-twenties walked in and sat down beside me. She ordered a double Manhattan on the rocks. When her drink was in front of her she pulled out a cigarette and turned to me.

"Got a light honey?"

I looked into her eyes. Deep sea green, wide and inviting. I fumbled in my pocket for a match. As I held the flame up to her cigarette, she touched my hand.

"Thanks, sugar." She slipped off her trench coat. She was wearing a short black dress with a plunging neckline. Her large breasts were half-covered, exposing one of the most beautiful cleavages my young eyes had ever seen. Luring me to her apartment was easy. I went willingly for a night of passionate, furious, feverish sex.

We entered the dark apartment. She pushed me up against the closed door and jammed a stocking covered thigh between my legs, hungrily devouring my mouth in hard, wanting kisses. I ran a hand up her thigh and under her dress, undoing her garters with trembling fingers. Her hot breath flooded my ear as we dropped to the living room floor.

At five in the morning she woke me from a deep sleep.

"Come on sugar. Rise and shine. You have to go now. My husband'll be back in the morning."

"Husband!" I shot upright.

"Yeah baby. He's on a business trip. But he might be back early. So best be on your way."

I was out on the street within five minutes. "Shit! I knew it was too good to be true. Damn straight women," I grumbled to myself as I walked home to shower and change before work. After that, I put her out of my mind and went about my life, working in the day, going out with friends and searching for a lover in the evenings. One night, about two months later, Cecile was in the bar again. I ignored her, but eventually she came over to me and sat down. She pulled out a cigarette and held it out waiting for me to light it. I reached in my pocket for a match.

"Come on sugar. Don't be mad."

I turned away.

"Come on Bobby. We had a good time didn't we?"

I shrugged.

"I didn't ask you to marry me that night, if you recall. I asked you to come home and fuck me."

I turned back to her. "Why didn't you tell me you had a husband?"

She shrugged. "I didn't think you'd come with me if you knew."

"Oh."

"He's away again. Won't be back till Wednesday." She put my hand on her left breast. I groaned. My breath quickened instantly. I was twenty-one and my hormones were raging. "Please baby."

I grabbed my jacket, her hand, and rushed her to the door.

For six months we met every other Tuesday. It was always the same. I'd swear to myself it was over, then she'd come along and seduce me. I'd cave in and we'd go to her place and fuck all over the apartment, our passion a runaway train heading for the edge of a cliff, momentum building to a fiery crescendo. Skin against skin, lips and tongue, blood collecting in swollen clits and raw nipples. Dangerous, impulsive, voracious, out of this world sex. The kind you read about in trashy novels, born of power and passion and impending peril.

Then, before dawn, I'd wake from exhausted sleep, throw on my clothes and she'd kick me out, teasing me with tongue and gaze all the way to the door. It was romantic, exciting, explosive and crazy. I loved every second of it.

One Wednesday morning, shortly before dawn, the inevitable happened. Hubby came home early to find his wife flat on her back on the living room floor in a half discarded black lace negligee with me on top, pumping away at her open pussy with my brand new strap-on dildo. We bounded apart and jumped to our feet. I hurried into my jeans and t-shirt. She reached for a black and red chiffon robe flung over a chair and casually slipped into it. He shouted at her and called her names. She lit a cigarette, blew smoke in his face and shouted back. He raised his arms above his head as he yelled. For a moment I thought he might hit her. Then I realized he was crying. He lowered his hands, covered his face and stood in the middle of the room sobbing like a child. Cecile went over, put her arms around him, pulled him close, told him not to worry, everything was going to be all right.

I left quietly.

The next day, I swore off straight women forever.

Madonna, k.d. and Cindy Crawford
1982, and wonder of wonder, miracle of miracles, femmes began reappearing in dyke bars. It was a sight to behold. Something was beginning to change. A new generation of dykes was coming out. Women who had bypassed the seventies. Women who had lived through them and come clear to the other side. Women who just didn't give a damn anymore about politics. Women who wanted to be sexy for a butch like me. The world was opening up and femmes were pouring out. Saturday nights I leaned against the wall in a local dyke bar, drinking beer and marvelling at the women before me. Women in dresses, high heels and make up. Women with long hair, low cut tops, lacy skirts and push up bras. Voluptuous babes whose bodies I could actually see. And all of them were dykes. No husbands or boyfriends. No closet doors between me and them. Just babes.

Shit-kicking, lipstick-wielding, shapely, curvaceous, romantic, mysterious, sexy, flirtatious, seductive, tenacious. Femmes. Women who make my knees weak with the toss of their hair, the bump and grind of their walk, the sureness of their stance, the invitation of their gaze and the soft round paradise of their cleavage. I had died and gone to dyke heaven. I was the happiest butch in the world. I hoped it would go on forever.

Now, Madonna reigns supreme, k.d. lang appears on the cover of *Vanity Fair* with the lovely Cindy Crawford straddling her legs, and everyday there are more and more femmes to behold. To be held.

I haven't seen my Aunt Rose in over three years. Not since the winter my bubbe died and we all gathered at Rose's to sit shiva. I found myself watching her when no one was looking. Now in her late fifties, Rose has aged with the grace of a fine French wine. I watched her flow through the house, majestically, and realized she was my ideal, the woman I measured all my lovers against. In my search for a girlfriend Aunt Rose was always in my mind. It was her style, her magic and her charm they had to live up to.

Sometimes life has a way of coming full circle and everything, just for a moment, makes sense. The rest of the time, I'm content with simple pleasures. The click of high heels on a hardwood floor. A short black skirt over stocking-covered thighs. A bra strap peeking out under a red silk blouse. The scent of perfume and soft, sexy whispers in my ear. My face buried deep in cleavage. The beating of my heart, the curve of her walk, the nobility of her charm. The femme mystique.

▼▼▼

Alex and Abraham

▼ In April of his seventy-fifth year, Abraham Rosenbaum rolled stiffly onto his side, gasped for breath and moaned. It was the same dream he always had. He sat on the hard bench of a leaky wooden row-boat. Behind him was Herman, his brother. In the bow were smugglers whose job it was to get them out of the country. He was seventeen. Herman, a year younger. Their older brother Shlomo had been instructed by their papa.

"I don't care how you do it," he said from his sick bed, "I want you to get my youngest boys out of Tiraspol, out of Russia completely. Before they turn eighteen. Farshteis?"

He left the reason unspoken. They all knew. At eighteen the boys would be conscripted into the army for a twenty-five year term.

For seven days Abraham and Herman hid in the bottom of a dry well. They held their breath while above they heard Russian soldiers searching for them. Silently, they shivered in the damp stench, tired, hungry, claustrophobic. Spiders and ants crept over their faces and down their bare arms. Nausea threatened to overtake them. Pressed against cold concrete, their backs ached. They waited and listened. Noiselessly they rubbed each other's feet to keep the circulation flowing and abate their terror. At night they climbed up to land and slept in an abandoned barn, high up in a hay loft. Before daybreak, they returned to the bottom of the well. Finally, the soldiers gave up searching and the boys were led to a tiny boat. Oars dipped into water deliberately, smoothly, quietly, as they made their way cautiously across the river to Romania. Silently the boys clung to a thin strand of hope to carry them across a deep and dangerous river. Their fate dangled precariously over a wide precipice.

The flap of bird's wings beating against leaves alerted them. Then the piercing crack of a rifle blast, followed by the buzz of a bullet so close its vibrations travelled through Abraham's skin. From the Romanian side, border guards. Instinctively Abraham dove, swam deep, far, dulling the thunderous clamour of shots. Held his breath. Touched bottom, feeling slimy mud, reeds and cold. He felt Herman behind him, against his leg. Down, down, down they pushed. Everything moved in slow motion, muffled, unreal, their sense of direction distorted. The ping of a bullet underwater reverberated nearby. Abraham felt Herman's hand slip away. He spun around. Where was his brother? His lungs screamed in pain. What happened to Herman? A moment ago he was right behind, clutching the material on Abraham's trousers. Abraham frantically whirled in all directions. Nothing but shadows, beams of sunlight, dark shapes. The current was strong and swift. It swept him downstream, his chest bursting in agony. He propelled himself upward toward the light blue sky. Broke the surface, gulped river water and air together. Choked, coughed, sputtered. Quietly.

Abraham woke suddenly. Breathing heavy, a cold sweat covered his body. He opened his eyes. Looked around. Saw the familiar radiator, pale blue walls, picture of his son Morris on his wedding day, in a white tuxedo, white bow tie. The framed photo of himself and Sophie on their fiftieth wedding anniversary. He saw his red plaid bedroom slippers lying on the blue shag carpet. On the bedside table, folded in half, was the latest issue of the Yiddish newspaper. A bright sun poked through cracks in the smoke-stained venetian blinds. After a minute Abraham's breathing calmed. He was safe. He was home. In the apartment on Bathurst Street. On the eighth floor. Beside him lay his wife Sophie, curlers in her hair, shmata on her head, sleeping peacefully.

Abraham sat up. There was something he needed to do. He slipped into his clothes, quietly, so as not to wake his wife, and left the apartment. He crossed the street to the shopping plaza and entered the Toronto Dominion bank. He waited patiently in line. When it was his turn at the teller, he asked for a thousand dollar withdrawal. He couldn't remember his account number. The teller typed numbers into her computer, frowned, and said, "I'm sorry Mr. Rosenbaum. It says here you're only allowed to withdraw fifty dollars a day. You need your slip co-signed by your daughter-in-law to take out any more."

"Vat?!" Abraham couldn't believe his ears. What right did Esther have poking her nose in his business? "Must be a mistake. It's my money. I put it in. I'm taking it out."

The teller drew in a deep breath. "I'm sorry Mr. Rosenbaum. I'm only allowed to give you fifty dollars."

"No!" Abraham shrieked, surprising himself. "I vant my money!"

"Mr. Rosenbaum." The teller spoke in a gentle voice. "Please, calm yourself."

"Crooks!" he screamed. "Stealing my money. Help!" Abraham heard someone shouting, but didn't know who. He felt hot all over. His face burned. He couldn't catch his breath, needed to sit down. But where? "I vant my money," the voice repeated. Abraham felt someone behind him. He shuddered. Did he hear shots? Birds? The rush of the river? He reeled around. A short man wearing a long white apron glared at him. He had to get out. He scanned the room. Lines of people everywhere. He had to find Herman. The man behind was in his way. Abraham wanted to tell him to move. He searched for the right word, couldn't find it. He was confused. And hot. Agitated. His head hurt. He strained until it came to him.

"Move!" he shouted, and with all his strength punched Max Stein, the neighbourhood butcher, who reeled backward and collapsed into the arms of Jason Brown, the young man behind him in line.

Peter Yee, at thirty-two the youngest manager ever assigned to that particular branch of the Toronto Dominion bank, sighed deeply, brushed a strand of thick black hair off his forehead, picked up the telephone and called the police.

Three thousand miles away in Vancouver, Abraham's granddaughter Kayla was sewing letters on to a banner with her local ACT UP chapter, preparing for a civil disobedience action. Kayla's friend Alex had survived three bouts of PCP, was battling CMV retinitis, a viral invasion which destroys the retina causing blindness, and his last test results revealed a startlingly low T cell count. There were several new experimental treatments for some of Alex's symptoms, most of which were not available to People With AIDS, because they hadn't been approved by the federal Department of Health. Kayla, furious at the government for turning its back on her friend, determined to do everything she could to fight.

Alex and Kayla had met in Toronto in high school. They moved to Vancouver together shortly after they both came out. Their friendship had deepened through the years. Alex was Kayla's best friend. He saw her through all her broken love affairs and failed relationships. They'd shared an apartment for a few years, but when Kayla fell in love with Jacquie, Alex found his own place and Jacquie moved in with Kayla.

ACT UP was gathered at Frank's apartment because he had the largest living room. Kayla sat on the floor with Frank, a tall, good looking actor who had worked in daytime television before he was diagnosed, Krishna, a middle aged ex-vice-president of an insurance company and Cory, a young bisexual activist and outreach co-ordinator at the Black AIDS Network of B.C. They were sewing the last few red letters on a long black banner.

Kayla used to work exclusively in women's groups, fighting for feminist issues like abortion rights and equal pay. When she started working with ACT UP a lot of her dyke friends yelled at her: "How can you put your energy into men?"

"If the tables were turned, would fags be there for us?"

Kayla couldn't worry about that. Alex was sick. He'd be there for her if she needed him. Of that, she was sure. As she sewed the last side of an "A" Kayla glanced over at Alex. He held a corner of material an inch from his eye, carefully stitching. In the old days, Alex was the best seamstress around. He custom-made gowns for half the drag queens in town. Now, his vision was so damaged from the CMV he couldn't even thread a needle.

By the time the police arrived at the bank, Abraham had quieted down. He sat on a hard green vinyl chair outside the manager's office, absently humming to himself. The disturbance was long forgotten. Over the last few years his memory had grown steadily worse. Sophie wasn't surprised when Dr. Pearlman said Avram had Alzheimer's. She had watched the same illness wear away at Mrs. Feinblatt, their next door neighbour, until she was a baby in an old woman's body. By the time she died, Mrs. Feinblatt couldn't speak, eat, dress or even go to the bathroom by herself. She wore diapers and laughed at things no one else could see.

For some time, Abraham had been forgetting things. Then, out of the blue, he started with the temper tantrums. Sometimes he was like a five year old boy, battling with Sophie as though she was his mother. The bank manager didn't know about Abraham's condition, though he had his suspicions. He told the police he didn't wish to press charges. But Max Stein, the butcher, had a purple bruise swelling on the side of his face. And he didn't like Abraham. Rosenbaum was one of those kvetchy customers who always complained and wanted only lean meat.

"I was minding my own business!" Max bellowed. "I left my nephew to mind the store and he's not exactly Einstein, if you get my meaning. I came into the bank to make a deposit like I do every morning and this is what I get? A punch in the face?" He turned to Abraham who, oblivious, was staring at a ball point pen he'd found in his shirt pocket, trying to determine its purpose.

"I want to press charges. A person doesn't get away with hitting an innocent bystander in the face."

The manager rubbed the worry lines deepening daily on his brow. "Mr. Stein. Are you sure you won't reconsider?"

"Throw the bum in jail!" He waved his hand and sneered in disgust.

The police obliged. Constable Christopher McLean, a rookie with one year of service, bent down in front of Abraham and informed him of his rights. He extracted a pair of shiny chrome handcuffs from his back pocket and was about to apologize to the old man for having to use them when Abraham jumped to his feet.

"Help!" he screamed. "Help! You're not getting me! Don't touch me!" Abraham mustered all the force in his seventy-five year old body and knocked the handcuffs clattering across the freshly-waxed linoleum floor.

That morning, the federal health minister was going to speak at the opening of the B.C. Medical Association's annual general meeting at the Pan Pacific Hotel. The hotel was designed as a cruise ship, with towering white sails and masts. Huge cement stilts supported it over the water beside the adjoining pier. The hotel and meeting rooms were expensive and extravagant.

The members of ACT UP dressed to blend in with the crowd. Alex wore a brown blazer, blue levis, white shirt and a tie he'd borrowed from Kayla's considerable collection. He looked like a student or perhaps a journalist. Frank and the other guys were wearing Krishna's suits, left over from his corporate days. Kayla dressed as she did every day for work in brown, pleated pants, a blue button down shirt and a navy jacket with the sleeves casually rolled up. Cory couldn't stand dressing up at all. She volunteered to be on watch outside the building. If the group was arrested, Cory would call their lawyer and meet them at the police station to arrange bail. If she saw anything strange, or felt they were in danger, she would warn them.

Inside the auditorium, they waited. Kayla sat forward in her chair and looked around, absently twisting a long black curl dipped over her forehead. People settled into their seats, nodded hello to friends and chatted among themselves. Some talked on cellular phones. Others entered data into laptop computers. Someone's pager sounded and half the room looked down at their belts. Kayla figured they were doctors, medical students, nurses, politicians, bureaucrats and journalists. No security guards were visible inside the room, although she'd seen several at the hotel information desk and one standing outside the front doors to the auditorium. The group had dispersed around the room so their action would have greater impact.

As the meeting start time approached, Kayla shuffled nervously in her seat. She'd been with ACT UP six months, but this was her first action. Up till now she'd only helped behind the scenes: sewing the banner, calling people on the phone-tree to invite them to meetings and sneaking photocopies and faxes at work. Kayla was no civil disobedience rookie. She had spent the early eighties in the streets with the women's movement, but it had been a long time since she'd been on the front lines. A few rows ahead of her, to the left, she saw Alex calmly chatting to May Chan, a progressive doctor currently in the news because she had helped five men with AIDS end their lives. Someone had leaked her name and she had been charged with "abetting suicide." Kayla wondered if Alex was telling Dr. Chan about the action. She hoped not. Alex had a loud voice and often wasn't aware how far it carried.

A technician walked onto the stage and switched on the microphone, tapping it with his thumb. A loud crackle and thump thump thump boomed from speakers mounted in all four corners of the room. People put away their phones, snapped shut the lids on their computers, checked their watches and turned their attention to the stage. To scattered applause, Graham Cunningham, president of the B.C. Medical Association ambled up to the microphone. In a dull grey suit and blue tie, he offered a few jokes, received polite laughter and some less polite groans. In a monotone voice, he read his end of the year speech, rattled off statistics, bragged about the Association's accomplishments and then quickly introduced the Minister of Health.

Victor Johnson had good stage presence. He was a smooth toothpaste commercial, big white teeth, bright sparkling blue eyes and a reassuring grin. In a perfectly pressed dark blue suit with a red tie, he resembled an American president or television news anchorman. Tall, wide-shouldered, poised and handsome. His hands gripped the sides of the podium authoritatively as he began to read the speech written for him that morning by his press agent, rehearsed earlier while soaking in the sunken bathtub in his suite upstairs. The crowd was perfectly quiet.

After the first few sentences, Victor noticed a young man in blue jeans and a brown blazer stand, smile broadly and step up onto his chair. A hard ball of tension gripped Victor Johnson's belly. Around the room people climbed onto their seats and began to chant: "AIDS death every hour. Blood on the hands of those in power. AIDS death every hour. Blood on the hands of those in power."

Victor Johnson's hands curled into tight fists. His teeth clenched.

Frank and Kayla hopped off their seats, strode down the aisle, leapt onto the stage to one side of the health minister and unfurled a large banner: Johnson's Budget Killed Our Friends. ACT UP NOW! Johnson stepped away from the microphone and snarled at Frank. "Put that away young man. If you leave right now, I won't press charges." Frank sneered at him and chanted.

Then Frank reached forward and seized the microphone from the stand in front of the health minister. "We are all innocent victims..." he shouted. "And we demand justice!

People are dying, while Victor Johnson plays with numbers. Services are closing down. Hospital beds filling up. My friend Jeff died in the emergency room hallway last month waiting to be admitted. Johnson's 'adjustments' are nothing short of murder...."

"My patience is wearing thin," Johnson hissed at Frank. A handful of condoms launched from Alex's raised fist bounced off Mr. Johnson's face and chest. The main doors burst open. Four armed security guards stormed in. One jumped the stage and dug his nails into Kayla's arm as he dragged her. She lost her grip on the banner and it dropped to the floor. A security guard pushed Alex roughly down the aisle. He stumbled onto the carpet. The guard hauled him back up, shoved him toward the door. People in the audience murmured, gasped and speculated among themselves. A young medical student stood and shouted, "Right on. Act up!" Frank managed to cram the banner under his arm while a man in a black suit wrenched his hands behind his back and snapped on handcuffs. The group kept chanting as they were led out of the auditorium.

"AIDS death every hour! Blood on the hands of those in power!"

In the back of the police car, Abraham settled into the grey vinyl seat and peered out the window. He recognized the synagogue where he and Sophie had been members for forty-four years. Small and orthodox, a little run-down since all the younger people like Morris and Esther went to the big modern synagogue. The windows on the front entrance were dirty. They needed to be cleaned. Why wasn't anybody tending it? He turned toward the front seat to ask Morris and saw the backs of two policemen. He shook his head and rubbed his closed eyes to clear his vision. When he opened them, the policemen were still there. Was he being arrested? What happened? He couldn't remember. When did he get into this car? His breathing sped up. He felt a pain in his chest. He unbuckled the seat-belt and tried to open the door but there was no handle. He searched for the window crank, found none. He banged his fists against the glass.

"Help! Somebody help me! Please. Call my vife!" he shrieked.

"Hey!" Constable McLean spun around. "Hey you. Stop that. Come on. Knock it off."

"Help!" Abraham frantically bashed his shoulder against the door. It hurt, but he had to escape. He had to. If he didn't, he'd wind up in a Russian jail. What happened to Herman? He was right behind. Sucking in short shallow breaths, Abraham smashed his brittle shoulder bones against the door over and over.

"Hey! Come on, settle down now. Jesus." Constable McLean turned to his partner. "Better stop the car Joe. I'll have to put the cuffs on him and sit back there. Jesus. What a crazy old bastard."

Constable Joseph Santiago stopped the car. His partner checked the safety latch on his holster and went to sit in the back with the old man.

In the elevator of Alex's apartment building, Kayla stared intently at the numbers as she ascended. The B.C. Medical Association had dropped all charges against ACT UP except one. As he was being dragged out of the auditorium, Alex had spit at the president. When the president found out Alex was HIV positive he insisted the police charge him with "attempted murder." They complied. Alex's lawyer was confident the charges would be dismissed in court, but there would be a trial. Kayla was worried about the extra stress.

Alex thought it was funny. He didn't have much to laugh about these days, so when he did, Kayla was glad. The daily treatments for his CMV retinitis were having a negative affect on Alex's T cell count. The choice was to stop the treatment and risk total blindness or stay on the medication and be even more vulnerable to a flood of other opportunistic infections.

"If Helen Keller could do it, I can do it," Alex answered.

Alex couldn't cook for himself any more, so every few days Kayla brought him cans of Campbell's Soup and bags of sandwiches, tuna or cream cheese on pumpernickel bagels. In the old days it was unheard of for Kayla to cook for Alex. He was a master chef, she could barely boil an egg. At home Kayla gladly washed dishes, Jacquie cooked.

At the police station in Toronto, Abraham Rosenbaum was Sergeant Tony Penchenza's problem. The Sergeant could feel a migraine coming on and reached into the top drawer for his prescription pain killers. He took a long drink of water with his medication and scanned the police report, every so often peering over the paper at the old man who sat in the chair in front of his desk, softly singing a song in a language Sergeant Penchenza didn't understand. Was it German or maybe Ukrainian? He checked the name at the top of the page.

"Mr. Rosenbaum," the sergeant said.

Abraham looked startled at the sound of his name, as if he hadn't realized there was someone else in the room. His eyes were wide.

"Mr. Rosenbaum," the sergeant repeated, more gently.

"Who are you? Vat do you vant?"

Sergeant Penchenza rubbed his forehead. "Mr. Rosenbaum? Do you know where you are? Or why you're here?"

Abraham smiled in an odd way and shook his forefinger at the sergeant. "You von't get me. You hear me. You can torture me if you vant, but you von't get me. No vay."

Sergeant Penchenza stared at Abraham for a moment, then rubbed his beard stubble. The old man wasn't right in the head. Senile or something. No point in pressing charges. Somebody should just keep a closer eye on the old guy, make sure he doesn't wander off on his own again. "Mr. Rosenbaum. Why don't we call your lawyer? I'm sure he can help us straighten this whole thing out."

"Hi honey. I'm home," Kayla sang out as she used her key to let herself into Alex's apartment.

"Well it's about time," he answered. "The kids and I are starving, the dog needs to go out and the Henderson's are expected over for bridge any second. Oh, and you haven't done the laundry and I haven't a thing to wear," he announced in his most queenish voice.

Kayla laughed, trying to collaborate with the playful mood he was attempting to create. She knew Alex well enough to know something was terribly wrong.

"Look what I brought — don't worry I didn't cook it."

"I could tell. It smells great."

"Hey. Be nice or I will cook something." She walked behind the couch, leaned over and kissed him on the cheek. He felt hot. She wanted to feel his forehead, but she hated it when she acted like a nurse — it made him feel like a patient.

"Oh god. Anything but that."

"Don't worry. Even if I could cook, I'm too tired." Kayla set a bag of take-out food on the kitchen table.

"Smells like Chinese food. Right?"

"Lucky guess." Kayla opened the cutlery drawer and fished out two sets of chopsticks.

"Is it from the place we used to go on Main Street?"

"No. I stopped at that new restaurant on Davie. Right beside the book store." Kayla carried two plates, cloth napkins, chopsticks and a bottle of soy sauce into the living room. "Do you want to eat right here?" She lay everything on the coffee table without waiting for an answer.

"I'm not that hungry," he said.

She looked at Alex and frowned. "Did you eat anything today?"

"Yes mother."

She went back to the kitchen for the food. "I got honey garlic chicken wings."

"You did?"

"Yeah and they make them great at this place." She sat beside him on the couch and opened up a container of steamed rice. "I think they deep fry the chicken wings first, then bake them in the sauce. So they're crispy, not mushy. Do you want rice?"

Alex didn't respond.

Kayla put the carton down and studied him. He stared straight ahead. Rigid.

"Alex?"

He groped the air around him, found her upper arm and held it. "I'm blind," he whispered.

The terror in his voice punched a hole in Kayla's heart.

When the phone rang, Esther Rosenbaum had just returned home from visiting her sister Gloria.

"He what?" she yelled at the police receptionist.

"He's been arrested for common assault ma'am. Sergeant

Penchenza recommends you have your father-in-law's lawyer meet him here at the station."

"What do you mean assault? Are you sure you have the right person? My father-in-law is seventy-five years old. He barely goes out any more. Well, except maybe to the plaza to buy a newspaper."

"Ma'am is your father-in-law Mr. Abraham Rosenbaum of Downsview, Ontario?"

"Yes." Esther answered weakly, easing herself into a chair at the kitchen table. Her back ached from planting petunias in the front yard. A sharp pain shot up her spine as she picked up a pen and took down the details.

Kayla was at work when she got the call. The voice was so weak and quiet she barely heard it and almost hung up, assuming it was a crank.

"Kayla?" a whisper.

"Alex?"

"Oh god," a groan.

"Alex!?"

Kayla could hear shallow, pained breaths. He groaned again. A thud and silence. He had either dropped the phone, banged his head or fainted.

"Alex! I'll be right there. Can you hear me? Alex? Alex!"

"Uhhh. Yeah," he wheezed.

"Just lie down. And stay calm. I'll be there in ten minutes. Oh god Alex, hang on. Oh god." Kayla snatched her jacket from behind her chair and dashed down the hall of the small publishing company where she worked. She paused at her friend Judy's desk long enough to say, "Tell Ben I had to go. It's Alex. He's sick. Really sick. Oh god."

"Kayla!" Judy yelled to her back, "Take a deep breath. Drive carefully!"

The black rainy road shimmered with weird patterns the entire ten minute trip down Main Street and into the west end. Kayla tried to focus on traffic, but she kept picturing Alex lying dead on his living room floor. In the back of her mind, she knew it was always a possibility. To remain hopeful, she had pretended the day would never come.

Sophie was in the kitchen warming a pot of barley soup when Abraham slipped out of the apartment again. From the lobby, he strolled outside and wandered down the street, staring at trees and cars. He passed a young woman pushing a baby carriage, two elderly women, one using a cane, her hand hooked in her friend's arm, and a boy popping potato chips into his mouth from a small bag. Abraham remembered his wife was cooking lunch. He was hungry and wanted to go back inside, but all the buildings looked the same. What did his apartment look like? He saw a white one ahead and remembered his building was white. It had a big porch on the way into the lobby, just like his building. He stepped up to the front door, realized he didn't have his key, and waited until an old man slowly climbed up the steps and opened the door. He nodded at the man who nodded back. Abraham followed him into the elevator and pushed eight, remembering he lived on the eighth floor. When the doors opened, he shuffled to 802. It didn't look right. Maybe his was 803. He crossed the hall. It still didn't look right, but Abraham was hungry. He tried the door. It was unlocked. Inside, a strange man sat at the dining room table. Abraham asked the man what he was doing there. The man yelled at him to get out. Abraham yelled back. The man rose from the table and moved closer.

"What's the matter with you?" the man asked.

Abraham didn't know. He shrugged his shoulders.

The man studied Abraham's bewildered face. "You crazy or something?"

Abraham felt like a little boy. He started to cry.

"Oh for chrissakes."

Abraham knew he was in trouble.

In Alex's lobby Kayla hit the elevator button over and over, then bolted for the stairs and raced up, two at a time. When she reached the eighth floor, she was out of breath. The muscles in her thighs burned. Her hands shook as she shoved her key into the lock and threw open the door. Alex sat upright on the living room couch, phone receiver still in hand. His face so white it was almost blue.

"Oh Alex," she rushed across the room and sat beside him. He was panting harder than she was. His forehead was burning. He clutched her shirt.

"I..." he struggled to speak. Every breath tore his chest. Sharp, deep pain. His fingers were cold. Pupils dilated. PCP again. He'd had it three times already. Aersolized pentamadine could prevent reinfection, but with Alex's T cell count so low, his doctor had advised him to take a break from the medication for a while.

"I...it just...started...so fast...woke up...with it..." he said between wretched breaths.

"Shhh," Kayla's eyes filled with tears. For once she was glad he was blind so he couldn't see her cry. "I'm calling an ambulance."

His fingers dug into her arm. "No..." he gasped.

"Alex why not? Come on. Don't say that. They'll put you on oxygen and give you pain killers. You'll feel way better later tonight. I'll stay with you. I don't have to go back to work."

"No."

"Alex, why not? Come on. You're scaring me. Want some water?" Kayla gently pried the phone receiver from his grasp.

"Don't want..." He started to cough, hollow, dry, racking. She knew he was saying he didn't want to go to the hospital. With trembling fingers, Kayla picked the receiver back up and dialled 911.

"Don't..." Alex drew in a rattled breath.

Kayla ignored his pleas. She didn't know why he didn't want to go. She felt helpless and scared. She had to do something. She requested an ambulance, hung up the phone and tenderly put her arm around his shoulder. She stroked his forehead, trying to calm him. She wanted to fetch a glass of water from the kitchen, but didn't want to leave him alone. God knows how long he'd sat on the couch. He must have completely dehydrated.

Kayla hummed a Yiddish lullaby her grandfather used to sing to her. She hadn't thought of it in years, but as a child she was always calmed by the bittersweet melody. She hoped it would soothe her friend now.

"Don't...go..." he squeezed out between laboured breaths.

"No, Alex. I'm here. I'm with you."

She brushed hair off his face. It terrified her to see him messy. He was usually neat and tidy, hair perfectly barbered and in place. Clean shaven. Socks the same colour as his shirt. Alex's lack of personal grooming signalled the beginning of the end. But Kayla knew she couldn't afford the luxury of grief right now. She needed to stay strong and do what needed to be done, singing and stroking his forehead while they waited for the ambulance.

When Abraham had been gone over an hour, Sophie phoned her daughter-in-law. She didn't like to bother Esther unless she really had to. Sophie and Abraham had lived with her son and his family for fifteen years before moving into their own apartment down the street. Often, during that time, Sophie had felt like a bother to her son's wife. The phone rang four times, then the machine answered.

"Hello. You've reached the Rosenbaum residence. We can't take your call right now. But if you wait for the tone and leave a message, someone will call you back as soon as we can."

Oy vey, thought Sophie. Vat's the vorld coming to? Now I'm supposed to talk to a machine, as if it vas a person. Who ever heard of such a ting? But if I don't, I'll have to keep on calling. She cleared her throat. She was always a little nervous using answering machines. It was like having your picture taken.

"Hello? Esther? It's me. Sophie. I'm a little vorried. Avram has vandered off again. He hasn't been home for two hours. I vouldn't've called. I know you're busy wit your own life, but I didn't know vat else to do. Maybe you'll call me ven you have a chance? I guess I'll try Morris at vork. So? Vat's new? You ever hear from Chava? She wrote me a letter a few monts back, but since den, noting. I haven't heard a vord. Is she all right? Is she still going to stay all deh vay in Vancouver? Is she ever coming back home..." Beep. "Oh." Sophie was startled. She was just getting used to talking to the machine. "I don't know vat deh beep means," Sophie said into the dead phone. "Is dat finished? Now vat? Should I call back? I didn't even have a chance to say goodbye. Oy vey. Deh vorld and me don't get along so good dese days. Avram?" she said to the empty apartment. "Vhere did you go? Vhere did my husband go?" She shook her head sadly as she put down the phone. "You're not deh same man. Not deh same man at all. Vat are ve going to do?"

Kayla wore dark glasses at Alex's memorial service. She'd been crying steadily for days, her eyes were red and puffy. She felt vulnerable and ugly.

"I look like a space alien," she told Jacquie in the car on the way over. Jacquie reached over from the driver's seat and held her hand.

Alex had made arrangements for the service when he was still in pretty good shape. All kinds of people showed up for the funeral. Members of ACT UP. People Alex had worked with. Friends of Alex's Kayla hadn't seen in a long time. Many looked sick themselves. As the gay Reform Rabbi droned on about life and death, personal spirit, grief and time, Kayla sat on a hard wood bench, wondering what she would do without her best friend. It was hard to believe Alex had actually died.

Sophie didn't want to do it, but she knew Morris was right. Avram wasn't well in the head. She couldn't take care of him by herself any more. He sat in the living room, on the couch, singing quietly to himself like a little boy, while she packed a few bags for him. The Jewish old folks home was just twelve blocks from their apartment. Morris said she could call a taxi and visit him any time she wanted to. It wasn't so much putting him in the home that was tearing Sophie's heart out. She knew it had to be done. Avram wouldn't notice anyway — most of the time he didn't know what was going on. It was the thought of staying all alone in the apartment. That terrified Sophie. In all her seventy-two years, she had never lived alone. When she allowed herself to think about it, she imagined sitting by herself, staring out the kitchen window. No one to cook or clean for, no one to talk to. Is that what life comes to in the end? An empty apartment?

Abraham settled in as a resident of Sholom Aleichem, the Jewish old folks home at Wilson and Bathurst. He didn't miss the apartment. He didn't miss his wife. Most days he didn't remember he had one. He didn't know where he was. Or how he got there. Life was simple. People told him where to sit. Where to stand. When to sleep. They brought him food. Gave him baths. Dressed him. People came to visit. Sometimes he recognized Morris and Sophie. Sometimes he didn't. One day, six months after his arrival, Abraham Rosenbaum slipped out of arts and crafts, wandered down the hall to a side door exit, opened it and walked out into a lovely spring day. The sun was shining. The snow was melting. Tiny daffodil sprouts pushed their way through the thawing ground. Bright green buds were beginning on barren trees. The sky was a light blue. The air smelled fresh even through carbon monoxide fumes emanating from the heavy traffic on Bathurst Street.

Abraham felt good. It was nice to walk in the sun. A bluejay nose-dived for a landing on a bare maple tree, chirping pleasantly. Abraham liked the bright blue colours on the bird's wings. He listened to its high-pitched song. Wanting a closer look, he stepped off the curb into the street.

Kayla was leaving for work when the phone rang.

"I'll get it," she yelled across the apartment to Jacquie.

"They say he died instantly," her father's voice cracked. Zayde Avram had been hit by a bus.

The truth was almost funny. Hit by a bus. Kayla stifled a nervous laugh. Her zayde, hit by a bus. It couldn't be true.

It was too crazy to be true. People always said you had to take risks because you never knew when you might get hit by a bus. Certainly Zayde Avram had taken his share of risks. A long time ago, when he was a young man, on his own, leaving his family, his country, his people, for an uncertain future across an ocean. Maybe he didn't take enough risks later on? If you don't, is that what happens? You get hit by a bus?

Kayla listened as her father told the story. She didn't hear much, but it didn't matter. Over the next few weeks she'd hear it over and over. As her father spoke, Kayla remembered sitting on Zayde Avram's lap as a little girl, watching him smoke cigarettes and read the Yiddish newspaper. Zayde Avram had been the wisest person in the whole world. Whenever she was troubled as a child, she always went to him. Even if she didn't have the nerve to tell him what the problem was, it was comforting to sit and listen to him sing and read, watch him smoke, turn the pages and shake his head at the news.

"Did you hear me?" her father asked.

"What?"

"The funeral — it's on Sunday. You'll come of course."

Sunday was three days away. Kayla said goodbye to her father and hung up. Jacquie wandered into the bedroom. Kayla was slumped forward on the edge of the bed, elbows on her knees, bottom lip sucked in, tears streaming down her cheeks. Jacquie sat down and gently placed her hand on the small of her lover's back.

"Babe?"

"It's a blessing in disguise," Esther kept saying.

Sophie didn't feel any blessing. She hadn't been prepared for this sudden death. She knew she would outlive

Avram. She had known for a long time. But she had prepared for something different. To visit him in the home, watch him wither away, go farther and farther from her. And from himself. Already, some days she could see the light leaving him, his liquid brown eyes turned inward, somewhere deep inside. Like a candle burning for too many hours, burnt to a puddle of wax and a stubborn wick, slowly fading to darkness. That, she had prepared herself for. For sitting on a hard chair by his hospital bed, stroking his forehead, spoon feeding him dinner, as if he were a child.

To lose him suddenly was more than Sophie could bear. Hit by a bus. What was he doing? Where did he think he was going? She thought about the accident through his eyes. The bus, speeding toward him. The panic he felt when he saw it. The horror as he was thrown in the air. Dead numbing silence of the moment he died. One minute she saw the bus rushing toward her, the next, she felt lifeless and dead herself.

Morris Rosenbaum lingered in the kitchen doorway and studied his mother. For two days she'd been sitting on the living room couch, day and night, speaking to no one, eating nothing. She didn't sleep. She sat and stared. Sat and stared. He tried everything. Left food on a tray on the coffee table in front of her, picked up the spoon to feed her. She ignored him. He offered her tea in a glass with a sugar cube to hold between her teeth. She ignored him. She drank the water he left for her and sipped at warm chicken broth, but everything else, she wouldn't touch. Morris kept the furnace high and wrapped a shawl around her shoulders when her skin felt cold. Brought her pillows and a blanket in case she got tired and wanted to lie down. Brought the phone in case she wanted to call a friend. Offered her schnapps in a shot glass, maybe it should calm her nerves. And she still ignored him. She did nothing. She said nothing. She sat and stared.

"Come on Bobby. Can't you do better than that?" Kayla shouted at her cousin over the phone.

"Sorry Kayla. Don't yell at me." Bobby Silverstein cradled the receiver on her shoulder and rubbed her temples. Kayla had been close to her zayde. It was a big shock to everyone, what happened to him. When Gloria called with the news, Bobby imagined Kayla's zayde under the big wheels of a Toronto city bus. It made her gag. She checked for flights leaving out of Seattle. Sometimes it was cheaper that way.

"Look. Kayla. I told you — you can apply for a bereavement discount. You have to get a copy of the death certificate and a letter of verification and then I'll fill out the application for you."

"Death certificate? Shit!" Kayla growled. "That's crazy. I need a piece of paper to prove he's dead? That's gross. He's dead, okay?"

Bobby reached for a large plastic mug of cappuccino — double tall — and took a long drink. "Kayla," she said, "I'll take care of all that for you, okay? But you have to pay the full price up front and then get reimbursed."

"Thanks Bobby. Sorry. I know it's not your fault. Sorry. I'm just — in shock I guess. I can't believe it. I was almost going to visit last month. Shit. I should have gone. How much did you say Air Canada would be?"

Bobby sighed. She felt sorry for her cousin. Her friend Alex died a few months ago. Now, her grandfather. She grimaced at the amount on her computer screen. "It's eight hundred bucks — with the tax."

"That's what I thought you said. I can't do it. It's too

much. I don't even have room on my charge card. Well maybe a couple hundred, but that's it. Shit."

"What about Jacquie?"

"Are you kidding? She's in the same boat. We blew all our savings last year when the transmission went on the Honda."

"Hang on Kayla. Let me see what I can do." Bobby continued punching in numbers, retrieving files and calling the airlines on the other line while Kayla waited on hold. Bobby was determined. There had to be a way she could help.

"She'll be fine. Just leave her be," Morris argued with his wife.

Esther stood by the stove adding a can of mushroom soup to a macaroni casserole. "Morris," she craned her neck around the door to examine her mother-in-law sitting on the sofa. "You've got to call the doctor. It's not normal. She's been sitting like that for three days. Twice a day she gets up and shuffles to the bathroom, but that's it. She won't even eat, Morris." Esther waved a wooden spoon in the air. Little globs of thick beige soup concentrate slid down the handle.

"She's suffered a great shock Esther." He reached for a bottle of kosher dills on the table and tried to twist it open. The jar was fresh and the lid was sealed.

"We all have Morris. But we can't just leave her there like that." Esther stirred the casserole mixture in the glass dish.

Morris picked up a knife and tapped on the pickle jar lid. He tried again, and with great effort pried it loose. "Aha." He pulled out a large pickle and bit into it. Drops of juice dribbled down his chin. "You don't know my mother," he said, crunching.

Esther dropped the wooden spoon into the casserole and spun around. "Don't know your mother?! Morris! I lived with the woman fifteen years. Believe me, I know your mother."

Fifteen years was nothing. Morris knew his mother. She was in shock. Upset because she didn't have a chance to say goodbye. She'd snap out of it in a day or two. He reached for another pickle.

Esther opened the oven door and plunked her casserole onto the bottom rack. "Morris. Please. Do me a favour? Call the doctor."

In the end Kayla didn't make the funeral. Bobby was able to book her a flight on Canada 3000 for $417 with tax if she left on a Monday or Wednesday. There was no way she'd arrive by Sunday, but Kayla reasoned her bubbe would need her more after the funeral, when other people weren't around as much. She wasn't expecting Bubbe Sophie to be in such a state.

"She's been like that for days," her mother announced casually. "You want some tea? I'll put the water up."

Kayla leaned against the living room doorway and peered at her bubbe. "You got coffee?"

"Instant."

"I'll have tea. What did Dr. Pearlman say?" Kayla slung her knapsack onto the kitchen floor. Her mother removed two Mr. Donut mugs from the cupboard.

"It's shock. He said to just leave her be. She'll probably snap out of it in a few days. Then she'll cry. Hopefully she'll talk. He also said," Esther lowered her voice and hunched down like she was hiding from something, "only don't tell your father. It'll upset him. That sometimes older people who have been together as long as your bubbe and zayde, go, one after the other. Like that." She nodded knowingly and took two tea bags out of a box of Red Rose on the counter.

"Go?"

"You know," Esther lowered her voice to a whisper. "Pass away."

"Oh god. Well, I'm going to talk to her." Kayla headed for the living room.

"Just don't expect too much. I don't want you should be disappointed." Esther held the electric kettle under the tap and filled it with cold water.

Kayla gave her mother a worried look and went into the other room. Sophie hadn't budged. Kayla sat beside her and took her hand. It was cold.

"Hi Bubbe. It's me. I came home to see you." Bubbe Sophie didn't move a muscle, except to squeeze Kayla's fingers. Kayla waited in silence. She saw a tear form in Bubbe's eye, watched it slide down her lined face, collecting in the creases like rain water filling cracks in a sidewalk. Kayla put her arm around Bubbe's shoulder and pulled her close. They sat like that for a long time.

The shiva was at Esther and Morris' house. Esther was glad Raizel still lived at home. With so many people in and out, she needed her daughter's help. Raizel cleared the table, set out food, kept a steady flow of coffee brewed in the pot, found people's jackets in the pile in her bedroom. People came and went all afternoon and evening. Cousins, uncles, aunts, co-workers. Avram's old friends Joe Finklestein and Yossy Levin came every day. Esther's sister Gloria practically moved in, her two oldest kids, Joel and Ellen, popped in and out. Kayla's brother Herschel showed up every couple of days. The neighbours came, Avram's rabbi from the old shul led the minyan, even the butcher, Max Stein, dropped by to pay his respects.

People went up to Sophie, who still hadn't spoken a word, kissed her cheek, patted her arm, gave her pitying looks.

Kayla watched her grandmother from across the room. Sometimes she sat beside her on the couch, holding her hand, saying nothing.

A few days later, Kayla was sitting between her father and Bubbe at the table after dinner. There were still lots of people eating, talking, clearing plates, setting out dessert. Somebody's kids were playing hide and seek. A little girl hid under the dining room table, her brother opened cupboards searching for her. Morris looked up from a piece of sponge cake on his plate. "You know. I think maybe it was the cough syrup that made him sick."

"Cough syrup?" Kayla snatched some grapes from a platter in the middle of the table and popped a few into her mouth.

"Yeah. You didn't know?"

"What?"

"He was addicted. Every day he drank cough syrup."

"He did?"

"I begged him over and over. Pa, stop with the cough syrup. But, he wouldn't listen to me."

Sophie gazed up at her son, eyes wide and held out one hand, palm up, fingers spread. "He believed in it," she said in all seriousness.

Kayla stared at her bubbe for a moment. She had grown used to Sophie's silence. The sudden change took her by surprise. She didn't know what to say.

Sophie winked at her granddaughter.

The night before Kayla was to fly back to Vancouver, she sat in the living room with Bubbe Sophie. Raizel came in, switched on the television, plopped down on the floor and changed the channels until she settled on a re-run of "Roseanne." After a minute, a commercial for the news came on. It was a clip of the Minister of Health, Victor Johnson, who had presented his budget cuts to the media earlier that afternoon. "Full details," the announcer said, "at six o' clock."

Kayla's body went rigid. Her stomach turned. Pure hatred filled her. The last time she had seen the Minister of Health Alex had been alive. The minister was slashing the health care services budget just like he said he would. Alex was dead, Frank was deathly ill, Krishna was failing and what little money the government spent on AIDS services was being cut even further. Kayla's eyes filled with tears of rage. The world kept turning, politicians kept lying, her friends kept dying.

"It's not fair," she said out loud.

"Shhh," Raizel complained, turning the volume up as "Roseanne" came back on.

"What mamelah?" Sophie asked.

"Oh...that guy that was just on." She pointed to the television. "He makes me mad. It's a long story, Bubbe." Kayla assumed that her grandmother was "Old Country," that because she could barely read English, she knew nothing about politics and didn't pay attention to current affairs. Once, years ago, Kayla had come out to her bubbe, sort of. She brought home her lover-at-the-time, held hands with her at the dinner table, introduced her to everyone as her new girlfriend and used the term "we" a lot when speaking about her life. Kayla was never really sure if her bubbe

117

understood, if she knew anything about gay people. Although she wanted to, Kayla lacked the courage to ask.

Sophie knew more than Kayla imagined. She watched a lot of television. Everything. The news. Barbara Walters. Phil Donahue. Geraldo. She especially liked that Oprah. Sophie knew all about pedophiliacs, agoraphobics, fundamentalist anti-abortionists and homosexual school teachers. She'd watched adulterers, pregnant teenagers, environmental activists, crooked politicians, bigamists, neo-nazis, lesbian mothers, women who hate women who love too much, transgendered people, people who have come back from the dead, Elvis impersonators and men who stalk women who reject them.

Sophie Rosenbaum sat on her son's living room couch, her heart weighed down with sorrow. Her husband was dead, but she was an old woman. And he had been an old man. Her granddaughter Kayla had lost someone too, Sophie knew, even though the girl hadn't told her. She saw the pain in Kayla's eyes, in the slow way she moved, in the lonely tones of her voice. She took Kayla's hand in hers and squeezed. The song Avram used to sing to their grandchildren began in her belly and rose to her lips.

Offin Pripachuck brent a fire-al
Un in shtib iz heys
Un da Rebbe learnet kleynah kinderlach
Dem aleph beys.

Kayla listened quietly as the familiar sad melody wrapped its sweet arms around her broken heart. She smiled at her bubbe and together, they sang.

▼ ▼ ▼

Love Ruins Everything

▼ "I think we should become non-monogamous," Sapphire announces over seafood curry at our favourite Thai restaurant on the Castro.

"What!?" A chunk of curried prawn lodges in my throat.

Sapphire lays her fork down. Sucks in a deep breath. "I've wanted to talk to you about this all day."

I swallow hard, trying to force the prawn down. "You have?"

"I've been thinking about it."

"Since when?"

She picks up her fork, plays with a piece of sauteed eggplant. "Since yesterday."

"Yesterday? What happened yesterday? I thought you went shopping."

"I did."

"For groceries."

"I did."

"At Safeway."

"Nomi. I did."

"And then you came home."

"Right." She stabs mercilessly at the eggplant.

"And while you were shopping you decided we should be non-monogamous?"

"Yes. No. Well…not while I was shopping. I don't know when. I just did."

I fold my arms across my chest. "Who is she!?" I blurt, a little on the loud side.

"Nomi." Sapphire nervously looks around the restaurant. "Lower your voice."

"Why!?" I shout. "I've got nothing to hide." Sapphire hates "a scene in public." Her WASP upbringing is deeply ingrained.

"Nomi. I won't discuss this if you keep shouting."

"Who's shouting?!" I yell. Both sweater-fags at the next table raise their eyebrows in our direction.

Sapphire tosses her napkin on the table and stands. "I'm leaving," she whispers. Everyone around us is listening, half-hoping she'll throw wine in my face or slap me. Make a better story for their friends.

"Sapphire," I laugh sardonically. "Come on. Sit down. You haven't finished yet."

She shakes her head, silently fumes across the restaurant and out the door. I signal the waiter.

By the time I pay, wait for my change and our remaining food — which I've asked the waiter to wrap up — run up the hill and open the door to our flat, I'm out of breath and dripping in sweat. I fling the bag onto the kitchen table. Sapphire is lying on the couch, in a knee-length t-shirt from Gay Freedom Day 1991. She flicks through the channels on television. Jody, her grey tabby, and "The Twins," Martina and Whitney, two pure black kittens she recently brought home from the animal shelter scamper over to investigate the take-out. I chuck it onto the top shelf of the fridge. Sapphire is watching "The Simpsons." I stand beside the TV and watch her.

"Are you going to sit down?" She's still angry. It occurs to me I should be the angry one.

"Are you going to talk to me? No one can hear us now," I say icily. It drives me crazy she's so uptight. My family screams and carries on in public all the time. To me, it's as natural as breathing.

She shuts off the television and makes room for me on the sofa. I sit cross-legged, facing her.

She takes my hands and gazes at me with a sweet, loving expression, the very look I fell in love with in the first place. "I don't want to hurt your feelings Nomi, I love you. It's just...I've always gone right from one relationship to the next, with no space in between. I've never really been single, and I don't know how to date."

"It's not all it's cracked up to be."

She sighs. "Maybe so, but I need to find out for myself. I don't want to break up with you. I just want to try my hand at dating. Can you understand that?"

I turn away from her and sulk. "Sure I understand. You're bored with me and you're looking for someone new."

She leans forward to look into my eyes. "Nomi. I'm not bored with you."

I face her, fold my arms across my chest. "If you dump me for someone else I'll kill you."

She touches my cheek tenderly. "I'm not dumping you."

"I'll shoot you. I don't care if I spend the rest of my life in jail. I'll do it."

"Come here." Her hands on either side of my face, she draws me to her for a kiss.

Three days later, I'm strolling down the Castro, a warm sunny afternoon in November. The fog has lifted for the first time in days. I'm supposed to be at work, but I faked a dentist appointment to shop. I'm carrying a bag of groceries, a box of croissants and cut flowers for Sapphire, all of which slip from my grasp and slide to the dirty sidewalk when a huge guy with a buzz cut, baggy pants and a baseball cap bends forward and french kisses my girlfriend. I stare at them. Everyone else stares at me.

"Hey lady," shouts an adolescent boy. "You dropped your stuff."

The lovebirds break apart. Sapphire's eyes are soft and dreamy. She's enjoying being mauled by this guy. I stand, transfixed, unable to move a muscle. The guy shifts to one side. Sapphire's eyes connect with mine. She stands up straight, at attention, like a kid caught smoking cigarettes or stealing money. I glare at her with pure contempt. She rushes toward me. Every muscle in my body tenses. I back away, leaving my parcels on the ground.

"Nomi," she yells. "Stop!"

I swivel around and stomp up the street.

"Nomi! Wait! Let's talk about it."

"What's to say!?" I yell over my shoulder. It's uphill and I start to breathe heavily.

"Nomi. What about your stuff? You can't just leave it here."

"The hell I can't." I know she's stopped to pick up the groceries. I don't feel her behind me. I march right past our street and keep walking. And walking.

"I knew it," my mother says when I call her in Toronto.

"What? What did you know Ma?"

"I knew it." She repeats. "I knew she wasn't a real lesbian." There is a tone of smug satisfaction in my mother's voice, like she just solved the bonus phrase on "Wheel of Fortune."

"Ma. What do you mean a real lesbian?"

"I always thought she was very feminine."

"Yeah? She was — is. So?"

"So? So, she probably really likes men."

"Ma, that makes no sense. Feminine doesn't have anything to do with it. Anyway, since when are you such an expert on lesbians?"

"I learned everything I know from you," she returns. "Oh and a little from Phil Donahue too. Did you see the show about lesbian serial killers?"

"Ma, don't start with me. Please. Are you listening? Me and Sapphire are breaking up. It's just like a divorce Ma. I'm very upset. I'm a wreck. I want sympathy. I don't want Phil Donahue."

Silence. I picture her nodding her head. "You're right Nomi. What was I thinking? I'm sorry. Can you forgive me? How are you dear? You need anything? Why don't you come home? You can stay with me. It'll be fun. We'll have pyjama parties."

"Ma. I'm too old for pyjama parties, and so are you."

"You're never too old for a little fun. Remember that mamelah. It's very important."

"I'm staying here."

"What's to stay for? Why don't you come home?"

"This is my home Ma. I live here now."

"Okay. You can't blame me for trying. So? Tell me. Are you okay for money? I'll send a little something to help out."

My mother the millionaire. We weren't exactly the Rockefellers when my father was alive. Now my mother gets by on a small monthly pension from an insurance policy he left her. "Since when are you so flush? What? Did somebody die?"

"Nobody died. It's Murray."

"What? He gives you money?"

"Watch your mouth young lady. I'm still your mother."

"What did I say?"

"He takes me out, three, four times a week for dinner, Chinese, Italian, steak, you name it. So, my grocery bill is a little smaller these days."

"Oh."

I can't bear to be at home. My friend Betty invites me to stay at her place.

"It's Sapphire again." Betty pokes her head through the kitchen doorway, holding the phone. "What do you want me to tell her?"

"Tell her to go to hell!"

"Did you hear that?" Betty speaks into the phone. "Uh huh. Okay. Yep. I'll tell her." She comes into the living room with two cans of Bud Lite, hands me one. I screw up my face but accept the beer and swallow a big swig. "How can you drink this stuff? It's terrible."

"You don't seem to mind." She sits beside me on the couch. "Want to know what she said?" With the remote control, Betty switches on her thirty inch TV. Stereo sound emanates from the speakers. She flips through the channels, stops at "The Simpsons."

"I hate this show." I announce bitchily.

She looks at me like I've lost my mind. "You love this show."

I shrug. "I hate it. So? What did she say?"

She hesitates, examines my face.

"What?" I say, unnerved by her stare.

"You're not going to like it."

"So? What else is new? Tell me what she said."

"She says she never meant to hurt you. She never meant to...are you sure you want to hear it?"

I beat my fist on the arm rest. "I said I did! Just tell me."

"Okay." Betty spits the next part out like she can't wait to get it out of her mouth. "She says she never meant tofallinlovewithRichard. It just happened."

This is too much for me. I leap up. A stream of beer shoots from the top of my can onto Betty. "Richard!? Richard! Just happened? Oh great! That's just great. It just happened," I repeat, as sarcastically as humanly possible. "How fucking original. Isn't that fucking original Betty?"

"Not particularly." She raises her butt, reaches into her back pocket, extracts a blue bandanna and mops beer from her face and chest. Her black shirt soaks up most of it.

"I can't believe this." I sink onto the couch, slam my beer can on the end-table, drop my face into my hands and cry. Betty leans over, rubs my back and drinks her beer.

I toss and turn all night on Betty's living room sofa. Next morning, Betty bounds in. "I'm going to Café Blue for a cappuccino," she says. "Wanna come?"

I drag the covers over my head. "No! I'm never going there again. Me and Sapphire used to go every Sunday morning."

"Well, it's Saturday."

Betty saves us an outside table while I go inside for drinks. Balancing two cappuccinos in one hand, a gigantic piece of chocolate cake in the other and a recent copy of the *Bay Times* under my arm, I squeeze through the narrow, crowded café. Almost at our table, I try to push past an unusually tall man. I look up, I'm face to face with Sapphire. The tall guy is HIM. Richard. For a brief second I consider throwing hot coffee in Sapphire's face. She knows what I'm thinking. Her eyes grow wide, she looks at the cups, then back at me.

"Don't you just wish I was that immature?" I spit.

She extends her hands. "Nomi. Please. Can't we just talk?"

"About what?" I thrust everything into her open arms. I don't look back when something crashes to the floor. Betty follows me outside.

Two weeks trudge by.

"Okay. So coffee was a bad idea. But you know what I would do?" Betty paces back and forth in her living room. She's nagging me to go out. All I do is mope around her apartment. I'm getting on her nerves.

"What?" I push a pile of silver paper clips to one side of the coffee table, brass ones to the other. Lately I've taken to sorting through Betty's junk drawers. It settles my nerves to put something in order, even if it isn't my life.

"Go out. Get laid. Have fun. Believe me, there's nothing better for heartbreak than sex. Nothing." She crosses her arms in front of her chest.

"What's this?" I show her a small metal object that might once have been a plastic keychain. It's covered in bubble gum so old it's melted. Underneath is a faint illustration of the Golden Gate Bridge.

Betty lunges forward, grabs the object and hurls it into the garbage can. I decide to go out soon, if only to make Betty happy.

Later that night, Betty goes out and I rent *Moonstruck*, the only movie I can stand to watch. I open a can of Bud Lite, pull Betty's brown and blue striped quilt over my legs and settle in for the evening. During my third beer, the scene I wait for begins. Late night in New York City. Loretta

Casterini and Ronnie Cammerari stand outside Ronnie's brown brick apartment building. A light snow falls as the new lovers argue.

"Love isn't perfeck," Ronnie declares. "Love breaks your heart. Love ruins everything."

I know the scene word for word. I speak the lines with Ronnie, with a thick New York accent, and just like him, I pronounce "perfect" like "perfeck."

"We're not here to make things perfeck. The snowflakes are perfeck. The stars are perfeck. Not us. Not us. We are here to ruin ourselves and to break our hearts and love the wrong people, and — and die."

A single tear rolls down my cheek. I never thought our relationship was perfeck, but I thought we had a good thing. I miss Sapphire, even though I hate her. As I drift off to sleep Dean Martin sings,

When the moon hits your eye like a big pizza pie,
that's amore.
When you dance down the street, with a cloud at your
feet, you're in love.
When you walk in a dream
But you know you're not dreaming Signora.
'Scuza a me, but you see
Back in old Napoli, that's amore.

I dream I'm in an old four poster bed. All around me are scantily dressed women whose sole purposes in life are to make me happy. One is kissing me. Another rubs my feet. Someone fixes me a drink. Someone else pays my rent. It's a lovely dream with a multi-million dollar budget, a cast of thousands, and all of them beautiful. Sapphire roams in, wearing a black negligee, slips into bed beside me, pours tiny kisses all over my body. Just like old times. I turn to face her and we kiss. She touches me everywhere with silk fingers. I feel a peace I'd almost forgotten.

I wake to keys jingling in the lock. Giggling. Betty and some woman I don't recognize creep into the apartment, trying quite unsuccessfully, in their intoxicated state, to be quiet.

"It's okay," I announce. "I'm not sleeping."

Silence, then, "Hi Nomi. Sorry to wake you."

"I wasn't sleeping." I drag the covers over my head as they make their way to Betty's room, one paper-thin wall over. I try not to listen while they have sex. With my head under the covers I'm in a cave. It's pitch black. My heart hurts. It beats cruelly against the inside of my chest. Quietly, with resignation, I cry. How did my life fall apart so quickly? Sleep creeps over the muffled sounds of Betty and her friend.

Next morning I decide to take Betty's advice. I've been crashing here for months. Last week we traded in her old green sofa for a pull-out couch and I began paying rent. I ask Betty for help getting back into circulation. Betty knows everyone. She fixes me up with Alison, a woman she works with on the gay and lesbian film festival committee.

"Oh. Did I mention she just came out recently?" Betty asks as I'm about to leave.

"What?"

"She's a little shy," says Betty.

Alison and I take in *Forrest Gump*. Halfway through the film I casually slip my hand into hers. It's nice to touch someone again but I'm acutely aware this hand is not Sapphire's. It's thinner and the grip weak. Tears roll down my cheeks as the movie ends. I pretend they're for Forrest, whose wife died, but they're for me. And Sapphire. Why am

I out on this date? I fake a smile and suggest a drink at The Café, a local dyke bar.

At the door, Alison is asked for ID. Suddenly I feel old. My life seems ridiculous. Why did I listen to Betty? I don't want to date. I want Sapphire.

"Alison, maybe we should just..."

The bouncer gives back her ID and nods okay. She smiles.

"What were you saying?"

"Nothing." We wander over to stools at an empty table overlooking Market Street.

We don't have much to say to each other. I'm new at dating and she's just new period. I scramble for small talk. The movie, the weather, our jobs, the community. After two drinks I'm enjoying myself. Maybe Betty's right. Maybe an affair would lift my spirits. I lean forward and kiss Alison. Her lips are soft but her kiss tentative. I shift closer, kiss her again. A quiet rumbling of lust stirs in my belly. It's been months since I've kissed anyone, three years since anyone but Sapphire. The DJ slides on "Mighty Good Man" by Salt 'N Pepa and En Vogue. We dance. I watch her hips sway from side to side. Her breasts round and full in low-cut spandex. She looks more attractive by the moment. I wrap an arm around her waist. We dance tightly together, her body against mine. She feels different than Sapphire, smaller around, a little taller and she moves slower.

I kiss her. Her tongue inside my mouth, soft breasts against mine, fingers in my hair. Rum and coke on her tongue. We kiss until the song ends. She grins.

"Maybe we should go somewhere more comfortable," I say. She gazes into my eyes.

We ride the Divisidero bus to Alison's small studio apartment on the ground floor of Haight Street, near Ashbury.

Her barred windows are covered in grime. Cars rush by, people yell, buses roar, music blares, panhandlers beg, dogs bark, footsteps pound overhead. The floor is sticky. Four hundred dishes crowd the sink. The apartment reeks of cat piss.

"Oh damn," Alison curses. She rushes over to the bed and feels the sheets. "Not again."

"What?"

"My cat's neurotic. Whenever I'm out she pees on the bed."

"Oh." I laugh, even though it isn't funny. "Come here."

She doesn't.

"What?" I say gently.

"Uh," she puts her head down. "It's just that...uh..."

"What?"

She looks into my eyes, hers dreamy with lust. "Kiss me."

I do. We kiss for a long time. We grope each other through our clothes. My nipples are hard. I'm getting wet. Desire pounds against the impenetrable fortress that seized my heart and body when I saw Sapphire kissing that man on the Castro. I ease Alison's jacket off her shoulders, toss it away. Undo the first small button on her sweater. Her hand grips my wrist.

"What? What's wrong?"

She looks down again.

"Alison?"

"Look. Maybe you'd better go."

"Go? But I thought you said..."

"I did, but I'm...just not ready."

"Not ready?"

"You know."

"Oh." I drop my hands to my sides. "Oh," I say again.

"Are you okay?" I try to see her eyes but her head is down and her long, straight hair covers them. Maybe she's crying. "Well, okay. I'll go then, uh, if that's what you want. That is what you want right? For me to go?" I want to move her hair so I can see her eyes, but I'm afraid to touch her. She nods.

"Well...ah...I'll...I'll call you. Okay?" I open the door quietly and let myself out.

"Don't be ridiculous Ma. Of course I know about safe sex." I sip from a steaming cup of coffee.

"Alright. I was only asking. Just in case, I picked up a few pamphlets at my doctor's office."

"Don't send pamphlets. I know what they say." Betty meanders into the room, passes the couch, heads for the kitchen, rubbing her eyes, stretching, her hair a mess.

"It's no trouble Nomi. A fifty cent stamp I can afford."

"Please Ma. Keep the pamphlets. Okay?" I hear Betty pour a coffee.

"What can I say? A mother worries."

"Don't worry, I know all about it. Anyway, lesbians are a low risk group." Betty trudges in with her coffee and plops down beside me on the couch.

"Mamelah, what are you talking about?"

"Ma. It's hard to explain." Betty raises her eyebrows and smiles broadly.

"So, try me. I'm listening."

"The AIDS virus is..." I grope for words, "more present in sperm and blood than...anywhere else."

Silence. Betty puts her ear to the receiver.

"Ma?"

"I'm listening. Go on."

I look to Betty for help.

A few weeks later BJ, Betty's new girlfriend, introduces me to her friend Mimi, a librarian, a few years older than me, also recently divorced. She still lives with her ex. I don't know how she does it. I can barely stand the thought of Sapphire, never mind the sight of her. I ask Mimi out.

I climb the steep wooden stairs of a pale green Victorian with large bay windows, fake front and ornamental trim circling thick white stone pillars. No one answers the bell. A television blares the theme song from M*A*S*H out an open window on the second floor. I ring again. I knock. I ring until I hear footsteps then nervously run a hand through my hair to smooth it down. The door opens. Mimi is wearing a silk, burgundy dressing gown, bare legs. Long wavy hair tied back in a braid. Beautiful, deep, soft, brown eyes.

I smile. "Hi."

"Oh, I guess you didn't get my message."

"Message?"

"I called to cancel. I'm tired. Had a rough day."

"Oh."

"Well..."

"Uh, well, would you like to take a rain check? We could go out some other time."

"Sure. Ah...what the heck. As long as you're here, we could go down the street for coffee."

"Okay."

"But wait. I've got to get dressed."

We talk over double lattés. Her life sounds even crazier than mine. She's spent four years with a big old butch called Nat, formerly Teresa Maria. They haven't had sex in over three years.

"But the first six months were great," Mimi stresses.

She still calls Nat "her partner" even though they broke

up nine months ago when Nat announced she was a female to male transsexual and had entered the sex change program at the University of California, San Francisco.

Mimi has been dating a bisexual woman named Wanda or the last six months, who also isn't having sex with her.

"I go to her place and we watch videos," says Mimi. "I come on to her and she says she's tired. Every single time. I don't know what to do."

I haven't a stitch of advice. "More coffee?"

We're having a good time, so we go for steak-and-whole-bean burritos at La Paloma Blanca on 18th and then to The Café for a night cap. After two drinks, she wants to go home.

"I'll walk you," I offer. She takes my arm and we leave the bar.

On her porch, I wait while she opens the door. She looks at me, reaches over and brushes hair out of my eyes. "Would you like to come in for a bit?"

"What about Nat?"

"Not here. Gone to visit her mother in Sacramento. She's going to tell her tonight."

"Tell her what?"

"About her sex change operation." She takes my hand. Hers is soft and warm. I squeeze gently. She leads me up a steep flight of stairs into a large two bedroom flat with ten foot ceilings. Over two bottles of Corona, we sit on a couch in the living room. A distant siren wails.

"So?" Mimi says.

"So."

She sips her beer. "How long did you say you and Sapphire were together?"

"I didn't." I gaze into her eyes. She smiles. I move closer. "I'd like to kiss you," I say.

She looks nervous. "Okay," she says.

I lean forward and put my lips against hers. I kiss her, but she just sits there. I pull away.

"Don't you want me to?"

"I thought I did," she sighs. "You're very attractive." She plays with my hair. "It's just that I realize I'm still in love with Nat. It feels wrong to kiss someone else."

"I thought you said you broke up?"

"We did."

"And she's a transsexual now, or whatever you call it."

"FTM."

"So how can you be in love with her?"

"I don't know. I just am."

"Well, Mimi." I grope for something to say. "Well. As a friend, that is — if I was your friend, I'd say you're selling yourself short. I mean, you said you haven't had sex with her for three years, and the bisexual isn't having sex with you either."

"Yeah? So? What's your point?"

"Uh," I laugh, unnerved by her building anger. "Well, nothing I guess. I guess I have no point. I guess I'll leave." I stand, hoping she'll grab my arm, say she's sorry, beg me to stay. She remains silent as I put on my jacket. "Well," I stick out my hand.

She shakes it lamely.

"Goodbye." Nothing left to say, I let myself out.

"Who says I'm depressed?" I'm sitting cross-legged on Betty's couch with the quilt over my head like a tent. Talking to my mother.

"Believe me, Nomi. A mother knows."

"Ma. That is so cliché." I lift the quilt at the bottom to let in some air.

"Are you eating?"

"Yeah Ma. Last night I ate a whole box of Oreos."

"You didn't."

"Okay. It was half a box."

Betty struggles to sew a button onto a black denim shirt. I've never seen a worse attempt. Jabbing her finger, losing the needle, sewing the shirt closed by accident.

"Give me that." I snatch it and start sewing properly.

"Why don't you come too. We're going dancing at The G Spot. It'll be fun. Maybe you'll meet someone."

"No thanks. I'm through dating. I'm no good at it." I twist the end of the thread into a knot and break it with my teeth.

Betty laughs. "You'll be fine. You just need more practice. Come on. I'll wait while you get ready."

I check the rest of the buttons on her shirt. "No. I'm going to stay in and watch *Moonstruck.*"

"Again?"

I fling the shirt at Betty. She catches it mid air.

Betty tries on different clothes, gels her hair, shines her shoes. When she finally leaves I slip *Moonstruck* into the VCR and settle down on my couch with popcorn, Dr. Pepper and Betty's quilt. Dean Martin begins to croon. The telephone rings.

"Hello?"

Silence.

"Hello? Who's there?"

"It's me," Sapphire says quietly.

Silence.

"Nomi?"

"Yeah. I'm still here. What do you want?"

Silence.

"I want to see you. Can I come over?"

"No."

"Nomi please? I want to talk to you."

"Why?" My heart pounds. Sapphire's voice moves me, more than I want it to. I put a hand on my rib cage.

"Can't I come over to Betty's? I want to talk in person."

"What happened? Did he dump you?"

Silence.

I laugh cruelly. "He did, didn't he?"

"Yes," quietly.

Silence.

"What do you want me to do about it?"

"I want to talk. I'm coming over."

"No! Don't bother." I hang up. Loudly.

Ten minutes later the doorbell rings. I open the door. Sapphire's been crying. I want to tell her to go to hell, but I can't. She looks defeated. I hold the door open wide. She walks past me. I follow. In the middle of the living room, hands at her sides, she gazes at me, eyes soft, full of emotion. It might be love. It could also be regret or guilt.

"I made a mistake Nomi. I don't know what else to say. It's over now. Please. I want you back."

I push past her, plop down on the couch, snatch my bowl of popcorn and hold it in my lap. "Are you crazy?"

Sapphire sits beside me. "Maybe I am. I don't know. I miss you."

I shove a handful of popcorn in my mouth and chew loudly. On TV, Loretta Casterini is fixing Ronnie Cammerari a steak. "Nomi...." Sapphire lays a hand on my arm, her touch so familiar it soothes and infuriates me at the same time. I look at her. She's crying. "I'm sorry Nomi. I love you."

My head feels like a helium balloon straining to float away. I don't know what to do. This has never happened to me before. I leap up, plunk the popcorn onto the end table and pace back and forth on the living room carpet.

"Let me get this straight Sapphire. You met some guy, fell in love, got dumped and now you want me back?"

She nods her head and grimaces.

I laugh and slap my hands against my sides. "That's great Sapphire. That is truly twisted. How do you think I've felt all this time? What do you think this has been like for me? You think I can just forget you dumped our three year relationship on account of some GUY? Some straight guy?"

"He's bi."

"Oh great. Even better. I hope you used condoms."

"I know you're mad..."

"Mad!? Mad? Are you kidding? I'm furious. And hurt. And humiliated...and lonely."

"Me too," she says. "I miss you."

I turn my back to her and face the television. With one drastic swing of his good arm, Ronnie Cammerari sweeps the dinner dishes onto the floor. He crosses the room, embraces Loretta and they kiss. The music swells to a crescendo. I face Sapphire. I know her so well. Everything about her.

"You didn't miss me so much last week. Did you?"

"Nomi. Please, don't do this." Sapphire's head follows me, like someone watching a tennis match, as I pace again.

"So? Was the sex good?"

"Nomi..."

I step closer, tower over her. "Was it?"

She bounds up and moves to the window, her back to me. Sounds drift up from the street. Two men laughing and talking.

"Was it!?" I scream at Sapphire.

She pivots around and glares at me. Sighs. "What do you want Nomi?"

"Answer my question. Was it good?"

"It was..." she frowns and looks to the side.

"What?"

"Different." She looks me in the eye. "It was different. Okay? That's all. Just different."

A vibration starts in my toes and surges through my body at the speed of light. I want her. I've never stopped wanting her, and I want her now. We hear the screech of car brakes, the unmistakeable crunch of metal on metal, a cacophony of horns honking. I stare at Sapphire, eyes set, determined. Wordless, I cross the room. She gasps. Her hand flies to her forehead like a southern belle, dazed from heat and gin.

Outside, someone is yelling.

I seize Sapphire by the shoulders, my lips on hers, hard, frantic, reckless. She moans, kisses me back, throws her arms around my neck. Like Ronnie Cammerari, I bend and sweep her up. Carry her to the couch.

"Nomi?"

"Shhh."

I am lost in the sweet familiarity of her body against mine. My desire is desperate, rash. Hands on her face, I devour her lips. Our first time and all the other times converge in one climactic moment. I reach for her breasts. She tears at my shirt. Naked, hands wild, desperate, flying on angel-hair wings to the skies, to the sea, to the beautiful sea,

You and me, you and me, oh how happy we'd be.
When the moon hits your eye, like a big pizza pie,
that's amore.

When the world sees a shine, like you've had too much wine, you're in love.

My fingers inside her. I know her so well. She moves circles on me, pushing and sliding. Soft and wet. Bury my face in her breasts. Warm, slippery, red fire. Fierce, longing arms hold me. Tight waves crash and break. We kiss. She moans. I feel her inside me. Searching, hungry, reaching for my centre, my heart. Oh honey, oh baby, I miss you. I want you. Body and soul explode.

"Yes, baby, yes!" Her hair in my face, sweet scent of her in the air, on my tongue, my fingers, my mouth, her mouth, my face. Her tongue on my neck, my ear. She bites my nipples, raw, sweet pleasure. Sliding in and out of her, of me, of my life. We bob on the sea, on the sea, on the beautiful sea, you and me, *you and me, oh how happy we'd be.*

She comes fiercely, head arched back, eyes closed, spirit open. Her fingernails scratch a trail to my ass, sharp, razor-thin strokes of passion. Longing. Desire. Home. *You and me, you and me, oh how happy we'd be.* Sirens wail. We lie still. I hold her. A man yells. The siren stops outside the window. A flashing red light circles the living room walls. We sweat. And we breath.

Ronnie Cammerari says, "Love isn't perfeck. Love ruins everything. Love breaks your heart." And I understand how true those words are. I love Sapphire. And everything is ruined. Our home, my trust, our love. I stroke her sweaty forehead, my other arm wound around her, intimately. I have no idea what I want to do. I want our old life, but I know you can never go back. The past is past. And everything is different now. I want to kick her out, make her suffer the way I did. I want to kiss her, make love with her, lose myself in her sweet salty kisses, her familiar embrace.

A key turns in the lock. Betty walks in. Practically drops her chocolate milkshake when she sees me and Sapphire naked on the couch. I smile meekly, embarrassed. She flashes a look that says she can't wait to hear about this, then smiles and heads for her bedroom. I squeeze Sapphire tighter. We watch the end of the movie in silence. I decide not to decide anything, tonight.

▼ ▼ ▼

Fifteen Minutes of Fame

▼ *Judy*

I don't usually drink in the middle of the afternoon. I don't remember how many screwdrivers I've had, but I'm definitely drunk. Took the afternoon off for a doctor's appointment. Had this flu for months. It gets a little better, then it gets worse. Thought I'd just been working too hard. When I went to my doctor's the first time he said it was probably stress, but just in case, he gave me a prescription. Then I got this dreadful yeast infection. Went back to the doctor. He said lots of women have that reaction to antibiotics and gave me a different prescription. I used the stuff for weeks but it didn't help. I was so itchy I thought I'd lose my mind. I went back to my doctor. He prescribed another kind of cream. I'd already laid out fourteen dollars for the first tube. I bought the second and faithfully followed the directions. Nothing changed. The infection got worse.

Another screwdriver. I've lost count. Must be my fourth. Think I'll stay here all day and all night. Don't want to go home. Don't want to see Elliot. If I did I'd stick a knife right through his heart, just like he did to me. I can't face anyone else right now either. What would I say? I can barely say the words to myself. When the doctor told me to sit down, I knew it was bad. Almost passed out when he said it. I thought I was hearing things. It just didn't make sense.

I'm a married woman. Never touched drugs. Okay, I smoked grass years ago when I was in college, but no needles or anything like that. And I've never had a blood transfusion. It didn't add up when the doctor said my blood test came back positive. I didn't believe him.

"Anyway," I told him. "I'm not gay."

Don't get me wrong. I don't have anything against gay people. One of my best friends is gay. No really, it's true. Kayla and I work together. For a long time I didn't know she was a lesbian. I guess we never talked about our personal lives — at least she didn't. Then one Monday morning in August, she came into work all excited and happy. She had the biggest grin on her face and was singing to herself.

"How can you be so happy on a Monday morning?" I asked.

"Because I had a great weekend."

"Oh yeah? Why?"

"It was Gay Pride Day."

I tried not to look surprised. I must have said something like "that's nice," but I have to admit I was shocked. I mean really, she doesn't look gay or anything. Or maybe she does and I never really thought about it. How can you tell if someone is gay anyhow?

That was a long time ago. Now we're really good friends and her lifestyle doesn't seem weird to me at all. I've been to her place many times. She lives with her lover Jacquie. The first time they invited me over I was so nervous, I circled the block four times before I had the nerve to park the car and knock on their door. I don't know what I was afraid of. They said to bring Elliot, but I didn't think he could handle gay people. Boy, was I ever stupid.

Kayla

Judy's been off sick a lot lately. She's always tired. We used to go out for a few drinks together almost every Friday night after work. Couple of times, I took her to Rosie's. You should've seen her the first time. I thought she was going to wet her pants she was so scared some big old diesel dyke would hit on her.

"You should be so lucky," I told her. "Women are shy. Mostly they stand around with their friends, drooling over good looking women, never doing anything about it."

"But what if someone does? What should I say?"

I laughed. "Just tell her you're straight. She'll leave you alone after that."

"Really?"

Judy is classically beautiful, in a Julia Roberts kind of way. Men are always hitting on her, and when she says no they call her names — bitch and cunt, stuff like that.

"Women aren't like that," I told her.

We sat at a table for a while, then I asked her to dance. She'd never danced with a woman before. I told her to just dance like she normally would. Once I got her out on the dance floor, I couldn't get her off. I'd never seen her like that before. Loose, relaxed, even a little sexy. She's not exactly uptight, more like reserved and self-conscious.

The last few months, we haven't gone out at all.

"I'm just so tired," she keeps saying. "I can't seem to shake this damn flu."

Judy

When my doctor first said the words all I could think of was how? How could I get AIDS? That's when he spilled the beans about Elliot. I was sitting in the chair in front of his desk, still in shock from the first news when he said, "I was hoping you'd test negative. Elliot assured me you'd been practising safe sex since he was tested."

"Tested? Elliot?"

"Oh no." I watched the doctor's face fall. "You didn't know."

I stared at him. Furious.

"Elliot said you knew."

No wonder Elliot was acting so strange when I told him Dr. Kirsh wanted to give me an AIDS test. I was worried Elliot thought I'd had an affair or something. Or that I was infected before we were married. Not that I was the promiscuous type or anything, but I dated a couple of other men before we started going out. I'd read that the virus can lie dormant for a long time. What an idiot I was. Can you believe I could be married to a man nine years and not know he's a homosexual, or bisexual, or whatever you call someone who sleeps with men and women? Not that we had sex much anyway. He was never all that interested.

"I love you for your mind," he used to joke. Now I know he really meant it.

I feel like such an ass. I can't believe Elliot would lie to me like that. Why didn't he tell me the truth? What kind of a marriage did we have anyway? It's all been a big lie. Maybe I'll get really drunk and take off to Mexico. What's the point hanging around here now? How can I face anyone?

Thank god my father passed away last year. He'd break both Elliot's legs and rip his arms off.

Elliot

Oh god. Dr. Kirsh called. Judy tested positive. She's going to hate me. I know I should've told her. Should have. But how could I tell her? We should've been using condoms. I know. I tried to bring it up, but she would've wondered why. She's on the pill. What was I going to say? Admit everything? Anyway, since I was tested we only had sex three times and I was careful. Always pulled out at the last minute. Figured if I didn't come inside her she'd be okay. When could she have been infected? Must've been before I knew.

I'm not gay. I could never love a man. I just have these urges. I find a guy in the park — there's a whole section of Stanley Park where guys meet for sex. I don't even talk to the men I've been with. Never tell them my name or anything. Whole thing is just a few minutes. Guess I've always liked a little on the side. Lots of men at the park are just regular guys, married and everything. Some even have kids.

Six months ago I ran into this guy I'd been with a few times. Steve. One of the few guys I was with more than once. I don't know why. We got along good. He was gay. Not married like me. He only went with men. He wanted to talk after we were done, you know, go out for dinner or a drink. I said forget it. I don't do that. Not that anyone would have suspected anything. But that's where I always drew the line. I only had sex with guys, nothing else. Never kissed a guy either. Well, other than Steve. He was the only one and I never meant to. It just happened. Our first time together. Didn't even realize until later when he said "Wow, you're a good kisser," or something like that. Anyway, it all started that day I saw him. He looked terrible. Skinny and tired. I knew right off he was sick. You can always tell. Before he said anything, I knew it was AIDS. I don't know how I knew. Guess I've seen enough pictures in *Time Magazine* or somewhere. Scared the shit right out of me. Couldn't think about anything else for weeks. From that moment my head started to pound and it hasn't stopped since. I made an appointment with Dr. Kirsh and had the test. I wanted to tell Judy right away. I tried to, lots of times. I just…couldn't.

Judy

Now I'm definitely drunk. Positively…oops I hate that word now, positive. One thing I know for sure is I'm not going to wait around until I'm wasting away in some depressing hospital room. I'm checking out while I can still walk and talk. I mean it. I'm going to buy a gun or something and when the time comes — well, you know. Oh god. Not a gun. That's too messy. Who would end up cleaning up after? Not Elliot, you can bet on that. Probably my mother, and I couldn't do that to her. Maybe I'll get some sleeping pills. Yeah. That's it. I'll get Dr. Kirsh to write a prescription and I'll save them till I have enough and go out just like Marilyn Monroe. Yeah, that's better. I'll wear black lace lingerie for the occasion and buy a set of red silk sheets. Get my hair done and a manicure. Open a bottle of expensive champagne and drink it out of fine crystal. Play Judy Garland records, lay myself out demurely on the bed and swallow the whole bottle. Wash them down with champagne. Maybe when they find me, I'll make the six o'clock news. It'll be my fifteen minutes of fame. What a joke. Famous and dead. Damn you Elliot. Why didn't you tell me?

Where's that bartender? I need a refill. Think I'll stay here for the rest of my life. I wonder if you can OD on screwdrivers.

There's so many things I haven't done yet.

Kayla

Judy's been off sick for two weeks. I've been calling and calling but she won't return my messages. I finally got hold of that husband of hers, tracked him down at the phone company where he works. He wouldn't tell me much, just that she's still not feeling well. She finally called me back today. It's a good thing, because I was just about ready to go over to her place and bang on the door until she let me in. I don't care how sick she is, that's no way to treat a friend. Besides, I think something serious is going on. I told her I was coming over tonight and didn't want to hear any arguments about it. She said she still wasn't up for company. I told her I'm not company. I'm practically her best friend. I'm going to stop at the deli on my way over and pick up fresh chicken soup. I hope she hasn't turned into a vegetarian.

Judy

Oh god, Kayla's coming over tonight. I don't know if I want to deal with her. I kicked Elliot out a few days ago. Woke up and there he was sleeping calmly, dreaming like he didn't have a care in the world. And I hated him. Hated him so much I couldn't stand to look at him lying in bed like that. Couldn't believe I hadn't kicked him out earlier. I should've kicked him out when I first found out about the whole thing. Must have been nuts to let him stay. I sat in bed for a while, watching him sleep. Hating him so much. I felt like getting a knife and hacking him up. The police would understand once I told them why. Of course I couldn't do it. I'm not a psycho or anything. But god, I hated him. So I punched him in the chest.

"What?" he leapt up in bed.

I punched him again.

"Hey Judy, stop!" he yelled, which just made me madder, so I punched him over and over again. Got him a few times real good in the face. He even has a black eye. I'll say one thing for him, he didn't hit me back. Tried to fend off my blows, but mostly he let me beat him until my arms were sore. My knuckles too. How do those guys in the movies do it? They never have bruised knuckles or anything.

We sat in bed not speaking for a long time.

"I hate you," I finally said.

"I know. I don't blame you."

"Well I blame you!" I screamed.

"I know, you should. It's all my fault."

"Bastard!"

"You're right. I am."

I couldn't stand how nice and agreeable he was being. It was disgusting. He was disgusting. I hated him. I looked at his face and felt nothing but contempt. I didn't want him in my house, or my life, anymore.

"Get out," I said.

"Judy..."

"You heard me. I want you out of my house."

"Judy please, let me at least take care of you," he grovelled. "There's nothing I can do about what's done, but at least let me help you now."

"No! I don't want anything from you. Ever. I want you out of my house. Right now!"

He held out his hands. "Okay. Okay. Okay. I'll go. On the weekend. I'll pack a few things. I can probably stay at Peter's..."

"No now! I want you out of here right now!"

"Judy, I have to be at work in half an hour."

"Who cares? Get out of here. Right now you bastard!"

"Judy, please be reasonable..."

"No! I don't want to be reasonable! I'm thirty years old and I'm dying because of you. Because you're a coward. Because you wanted it all. Well you can't have it all. Not anymore. So get out!"

"Judy..."

"I mean it Elliot. I'm going to get a frying pan from the kitchen if you don't get out."

He finally left. I was happy to see him go.

I can't stand to look at him any more.

Kayla

At first Judy wouldn't tell me what was the matter. She tried to act cheerful, like everything was okay, but I kept pouring red wine into her glass. Eventually I wore her down. I can't believe it. She's straight. This wasn't supposed to happen to a straight friend. I knew I would probably go through it again with someone. Maybe Krishna or one of the other guys in ACT UP, but I never expected Judy. I picked up my wine glass. My hands were shaking. She misunderstood. She thought I was freaked out, like I couldn't handle it or something. I reminded her about Alex. I never told her much about him at the time — she'd just started working at Brown and Dumphries the year Alex died. We were just getting to know each other. Judy closed her eyes and shook her head.

"Sorry. I forgot."

I put my hand on her arm.

We sat in silence for a moment. I could see her mind darting all over the place. She looked terrified, then almost resigned. "Everybody dies, don't they? It's just a matter of time now."

"I know a guy who's been living with AIDS for ten years," I told her, wanting to fill her with enough hope to get through the first round. I told her if it ever gets really rough she can move in with me and Jacquie and we'll take care of her. When I said that, she leaned over the kitchen table, put her head in her hands and started to cry.

"That's it," I said, rubbing her back, "Let it out."

She asked me why I was being so nice.

"For god's sake Judy," I said. "What did you expect?"

She shrugged.

"You don't have to go through this all alone," I told her, which only made her cry even more.

I picked up her wine glass by mistake and took a sip.

"No!" she lunged for it, knocking it out of my hands, the red wine splattering down the front of my white shirt, the glass shattering on the floor. "I drank from that!" Her eyes were wide with panic.

I told her it didn't matter. You can't catch it that way.

"Oh god." She chewed on her thumbnail. "You're right. I'm sorry. It's...I feel...oh god. I feel so...contagious." She held out her hands and studied her palms.

I picked up the glass carefully, wrapped it in a plastic bag and placed it in the garbage. Alex had said the same thing. He worried that people were afraid of him. Afraid to touch him.

"Remember who you're talking to," I reminded her. "I'm not the general public. I'm not afraid."

I poured her more wine in a fresh glass and stayed with her until she said she was tired. She's thinking of quitting work. We have a long term disability plan. I told her it was a good idea.

Elliot

Damn couch I've been sleeping on is too short. My legs stick off the end. I wake up all the time with cramps, or pins and needles from where the edge has been digging into my calves. Judy won't speak to me at all. Won't return my calls. I asked Peter to call her for me and tell her I want to talk. He won't do it. Doesn't want to get involved. I didn't tell him why she threw me out. I can't. He might not let me stay if he knows about me, and I can't afford to get a place of my own. I'm still paying half the mortgage on the condo. If I don't, Judy'll have to move. No matter what she thinks, I still care about her. I never meant to hurt her. Damn. If I'd known. If I'd only known. If I could've done it differently, I would've. Judy thinks I'm a creep. She doesn't know. She can never know what it's like to have desires for other men and want to be normal. That's all I ever wanted — to be normal. It started in high school. Seemed like it creeped up on me a little at a time. The sight of George, the boy next door, mowing the lawn bare chested. The ads in the back of comics — you know — Charles Atlas, muscle man. I found my sister's secret stash of *Playgirl*. Stole a couple copies. Would lock myself in the bathroom and jerk off. I could hardly handle the locker room at school. Learned to keep my eyes down, think about my mother or math homework, otherwise I'd get a boner for sure just looking at the other guys getting undressed, showering.

I went out with girls. Lots of them. I was pretty popular. Never touched one of them. They thought I was the perfect gentleman. When I met Judy I knew right away I wanted to marry her. She's, I don't know, she's got character. She's smart and she's...well, she's real. You know, not like some of the girls I went out with, who acted like they were helpless or something. Judy was never like that. I'm not a fag. That's what everyone would call me if they knew. If the guys at work knew about me they'd think I was a freak. I'd have no friends.

For a while it seemed everything would work out. I was a good husband. Did my share of the dishes and the cleaning. Did all the laundry and the guy stuff too — taking out the trash, fixing the toilet. Judy and I had season's tickets for the Queen Elizabeth Theatre. Okay, they weren't the greatest seats in the house, but we saw all the shows. Shit, we even started talking about having a kid. God! A kid. Man, good thing we waited on that. What a mess that would have been.

Crazy part is, I'm not sick at all. I'm healthy as a horse. Don't even catch colds. I read in a magazine that HIV might not even be the thing that causes AIDS anyway. There's lots of people been walking around for years and aren't sick yet. You just got to maintain a positive attitude and not let the fucking thing get the better of you.

If Judy would just return my calls.

Judy

I've been off work almost a year. It's a miracle I'm still alive. When I was first diagnosed I thought I'd be dead in six months, but here I am walking, talking, breathing. Sometimes I feel okay. The rest of the time I feel lousy, but I'm still here. Sort of. I was in bad shape most of last month. Damn yeast infection keeps coming back. And I just don't have much energy. I joined this group called Positive Women at the PWA society downtown. There's six other women in the group who got it the same way as me. *Six.* Can you believe that? And Marnie, the leader, says there's probably hundreds of others we don't know about. Apparently lots of married men have sex with other men on the sly. Nobody would've ever known except for AIDS. Sometimes for therapy we draw pictures of our husbands. Then we scribble all over them and rip them to shreds. One day I put my shreds in an envelope and mailed them to Elliot. I didn't sign it or anything. Just sent it to Peter's address.

Thank god for Kayla. She's been my best friend through this whole thing. The only one who doesn't ask stupid questions. People who don't have AIDS just don't understand. Everyone wants to know how I got infected. It doesn't matter. What matters is how to stay healthy. They want to know about dying, or they don't want to know, and tiptoe around me so carefully it makes me laugh. I've already gone through the whole thing about dying. I know it's going to happen. I've already decided. As soon as the pain is too much, or I can't take care of myself anymore, I'm out of here. I'm stockpiling pills. Dr. Kirsh keeps renewing my prescription and I keep stashing the bottles in my bedside table. Everything's all taken care of for after I go. I wrote down what I want for my memorial service and everything. It's in a safety deposit box at the bank. I'm thinking about asking Kayla to take care of things when I'm gone.

Last month when I was really sick, she stayed over for a few nights in the spare room. I was afraid to ask, but she offered.

Didn't want to leave me alone in case I needed something. I don't know what I'd do without her.

Kayla

Sometimes it's hard to be around Judy. She makes me think about Alex. I can't believe it's already four years since he died. Where did the time go? When he first died I didn't know how to live in a world without him. But you do. You go on. It wouldn't be so bad if he'd been the only one, or if Judy was. I can't tell you how many friends I've lost. Ten, twelve, fourteen. I don't know. I'd have to write their names on a piece of paper or I'm sure I'd forget someone.

Judy watches that same stupid show Alex used to watch — *Star Trek*. One night when I was a little stoned on grass I wondered if *Star Trek* was a co-factor — you know, they're always talking about co-factors to HIV, like poppers, antibiotics, prior STDs. I never understood the big attraction to

Star Trek. Always seemed boring in a Walt Disney kind of way. Baffled me that people I call friends would watch drek like that. Except now. Sometimes I find myself switching the damn show on. Nostalgia I think. It reminds me of Alex. I never believed in reincarnation until all my friends started dying. Now I hang on to the idea as if my life depended on it. I don't miss them as much that way. It's like they're still here, in a different form. Sometimes I feel Alex hanging around. Not at my place. He wouldn't know where this apartment is. We moved here two years after he died. But at work sometimes, in the office. I swear I hear him behind me. Not out loud, more like inside my head. I hear my name being called, and memories, all different ones, flood through me. I smell things, hear them, taste even. It's weird. One time it was won ton soup. I was standing at the Xerox machine photocopying fliers when I had an overwhelming taste of barbecue pork won ton noodle soup in the back of my throat, the kind Alex and me used to take out from the Szechuan at Granville and Davie. We'd add so much hot chili pepper we'd both be coughing and crying. Our mouths burning. We'd wash it down with bottles of Evian Alex always had in his fridge. It's crazy the things you think about.

Jacquie and I've been fighting a lot lately. I think she's jealous. Not that there's anything romantic between me and Judy. Jacquie's just jealous about how much time I spend over there.

"I don't have all the time in the world. She won't be around that much longer," I explained.

"So? What about me?" Jacquie said. "I could get hit by a truck tomorrow."

"Jacquie. Don't say that." I'm a little superstitious. That's how my zayde died — hit by a bus. It drives me crazy when

Jacquie says stuff like that. Gives me chills. Jacquie's never had a friend die on her, so she doesn't understand. I'm trying to be patient, but it's hard. We were living together while Alex was dying. She was there for most of it. She should know how fast it can happen. Once someone is gone, they're gone. I wish Jacquie would try to see my point of view.

Judy

Last week in the middle of the night I had to call Kayla. The doctors still don't know what it was. Something happened in my brain. I woke up and couldn't move a muscle. I could open my eyes, but nothing else. It stayed like that for the whole day. I was conscious, but couldn't move. Kept falling asleep and waking up. I started to get scared. Hot and cold with fever. I knew if I stayed like that too long, I'd die. I wished I had a room-mate, someone who might eventually find me on their way to the bathroom. I even cursed myself for kicking Elliot out. Friends would probably phone, but I had the answering machine on. They'd think I just didn't have the energy to call back. It would be days before someone got worried enough to check on me. When the sun began to go down, I could feel tingling in my fingers. I put every ounce of strength into trying to move my hand. It took hours. Finally I could move just enough to get the phone and punched the button for Kayla's number — I have it set on the auto dialler. It must have been four in the morning but she came right over, called an ambulance and came with me to the hospital. Now I can move again. Whatever was wrong stopped. The doctor wants me to stick around for a while. He says I'm dehydrated and wants to do some blood work. "As long as you're here, we might as well," he said. I felt like a car in the shop.

"Yep, as long as the hood's up, you might as well check the oil," I said.

Dr. Kirsh laughed. He's starting to get used to my morbid sense of humour.

Elliot

Yesterday I slept so late, didn't get to work till eleven. Boss called me in. Third time in two weeks I've been late. She wanted to know have I been drinking or something, and how's my personal life and all that. I told her everything is fine, thank you. Had my employee record on the desk in front of her. I could tell that's what it was, 'cause I could see my name on the outside. She gave me one of those "you have a good record so I'll overlook this but you'd better pick it up in the future" speeches.

"You bet," I promised.

I'm just so damn tired these days. All I want to do is sleep. Last Friday, Peter and some of the guys invited me to this party. Sounded like a great idea early in the day, but after supper I fell asleep on the couch. Peter says he tried to wake me, but I was knocked out. Slept right through until dinner the next day. Don't know what's wrong with me. Just can't seem to perk up.

I hear Judy's become some kind of political type, belongs to a group at the AIDS centre. I just hope she's using her maiden name. Don't want anyone there to know about me. She's probably the only woman in the whole place. Rest of them are probably fags. Peter says I should get a lawyer. That I don't have to keep paying the mortgage if I'm not going to live there, but I can't do that to Judy. I hear she's not doing so good these days.

Kayla

I finally talked to Jacquie about letting Judy move into the guest room. She can't stay in that condo by herself much longer. Jacquie said no at first, but she could see how much it meant to me and finally gave in. I'm not sure how to bring it up to Judy. She gets embarrassed when I take care of her. She has other friends, but I think they're scared. I've been through this already with Alex. It wrenches my heart, but it doesn't scare me.

Judy

Maybe it's time to buy that black lingerie and do my Marilyn Monroe routine. I've got enough pills saved up, I think. I don't know. How much is enough?

▼ ▼ ▼

A Working Dyke's Dream

▼ When I first started working at Gulliver's Travel my boss was a balding, middle-aged man named Seymour Plotkin. Two months ago, Seymour had a nervous breakdown after his wife ran off with their gardener. For a week I didn't have a boss. The following Monday I was sitting at my computer when the front door opened. I heard footsteps approaching and looked up at a beautiful woman standing in front of my desk. Smiling right at me. I smiled back as she offered her hand.

"Hi," she said, "I'm Sadie Singer, the new manager."

I knew I was supposed to stand up, shake her hand, introduce myself, all that normal stuff, but I couldn't take my eyes off her soft full lips, or her finely sculpted cheekbones. Her powerful gaze melted my Monday morning haze. With gargantuan effort I raised my hand and took hers, desperately forcing a business-like handshake, when I really felt like lifting her hand to my lips and planting a tender kiss on her smooth olive skin. My knees shook as I pushed my steno chair backward and stood. I was slightly taller. My eyes met hers. She was a goddess. A short, voluptuous, brown-eyed, frizzy-haired movie star who walked right off the pages of *People* magazine and into Gulliver's Travel.

"You must be Barbara Silverstein..." she said in a husky, ex-smoker's voice.

"Please," I begged, "call me Bobby. Everyone does."

She held my hand a beat longer than necessary. "Alright...Bobby." She smiled and dropped my hand. It plunged to earth and hung at my side, fingers vibrating from her touch. I stared into her eyes, silently thanking whatever higher power had caused Mr. Plotkin's wife to run off with a younger man so I could be blessed with a boss like Sadie Singer. A working dyke's dream. A boss who looked like Bette Midler, Madonna, Jessica Lange, and Queen Latifah all rolled into one. Instead of answering "yes sir" to a middle-aged man, I would now be "yes ma'aming" a Hollywood bombshell.

"Bobby, why don't you show me around. Then I'd like to organize my office. I understand Mr. Plotkin left in a hurry and things are in some disarray."

Yes ma'am, please allow me to show you the inside of the supply cupboard, or better yet my apartment, I wanted to say. "There's not much to show," I said instead. "We're pretty small. Just me, Jack — he's off sick today — and Jerry over there." I pointed to my co-worker, a flamboyant drag queen dressed as butch as he could to make a living in the business world. Still, he looked like Diana Ross in a three-piece suit, or an older Michael Jackson. Butch and femme at the same time.

I led the way to introduce Sadie to Jerry. She followed so closely I could almost feel her nipples pressing against my back. It was growing warmer in the office. I undid the top button of my shirt.

As we approached Jerry stood, stuck out his hand and half-curtsied. "Well, at least you dress better than poor old Mr. Plotkin. No wonder his wife left him."

"Thank you Jerry," Sadie laughed. "I'll take that as a compliment."

I led my new boss to the lunchroom, which had a small fridge, a coffee machine and a table and chairs. At the very back was an oversized closet which we called the supply room. Inside, I began pointing out the elaborate inventory system Mr. Plotkin had set up. There were stacks of vacation brochures, corporate flight planners, and travel insurance folders. I had my back to Sadie as I opened drawers and cupboards to let her see inside. When I turned her eyes were all over my body. For a moment I didn't know if she was straight or gay. A fine sweat formed on my skin and I casually rolled my shirt sleeves up to my elbows. I spent a long time explaining where we ordered Xerox paper from, while in my mind I saw myself leaning her up against the shelves and opening her buttons, one by one, until her beautiful voluptuous breasts leapt out at me. Silently, she would guide my hand underneath her skirt and I would feel her wetness calling me up inside of her, and there, in the closet, I would plunge my fingers into her and she would urge me on and on until she was coming and calling out my name. Her back would be indented by stacks of Club Med brochures, but she wouldn't care. She'd lean back after and have a cigarette. Maybe give me a raise and invite me home to dinner.

"Fine." Her voice came out of nowhere. "I think we've covered the supply room quite sufficiently."

"Right," I agreed, wiping the sweat from my forehead.

Somehow I made it back to my desk without laying a hand on her. She went into her glass-enclosed office and began going through files. I had a clear view of her from where I sat. Each time she reached for a manila folder on her desk she had to bend slightly, teasing me with the sight of her ample cleavage. Every so often she'd glance in my direction. I was sure she was checking me out too. I pretended to enter words into my keyboard. I shuffled papers from one side of my desk to the other. All the while I had one eye on Sadie and the other turned inward, enjoying fantasies inside my head.

All morning I was a one-woman porn production company. I'd have made a fortune in the X-rated movie business if I could have captured those images on film. By lunchtime I had seduced my sexy boss in every inch of the office, kissed, fondled and fucked her on every available desk, photocopier, and fax machine. In my mind.

At noon, I kept one eye on Sadie as she casually freshened her lipstick. The care she was taking with her appearance meant she must be meeting someone. I pretended to concentrate deeply on the flight information on my monitor as she whisked past me, saying she'd be back at one o'clock.

"You bet," I grinned. "See you then." When she couldn't see, I took the opportunity to devour her from behind. So femme I almost died at the sight. I could swear she wore old-fashioned stockings with a seam up the back. Her perfume wafted into my nose and I swooned, breathing her womanly scent deeply. Her ass was perfect, just how derrieres were meant to be — round, full and big. It bounced and danced from side to side as she sauntered out the glass door and into the street. I felt like a teenage boy who'd just glimpsed Marilyn Monroe. My heart raced, my palms sweated, my eyes sang a hundred rhapsodies to her. The second she was gone, I switched off my screen, snatched my jacket, and yelled back to Jerry. "See you at one. Out for lunch."

"Better watch out, girlfriend," I heard him call as I

dashed for the door. "Business and pleasure are like oil and water. Take it from me."

There are times in a dyke's life when she just has to be crazy. There's no accounting for it. It happens out of the blue, on days that start out like any other. I was just this side of something reckless, but couldn't stop myself. I was out in the street. Ahead of me I could see Sadie. I stayed close to the wall. If she turned around, I could duck into the nearest shop. I didn't want her to see me, but I wanted to see who she was meeting. Woman or man? Husband? Lover? Friend? I needed to know if she was straight or gay or what. I didn't stop to think about how ridiculous I was being. There was no time for that. I didn't want to lose her.

At the skytrain station she took the escalator down to the mall under the office towers to the fast food fair, where pizza, Chinese food and falafel stands surrounded hundreds of orange tables and yellow plastic chairs. Between noon and one on a weekday the place is packed. Perfect. I could find a seat far enough away to be hidden, yet close enough to see what Sadie was up to. Keeping a respectable distance, I followed her down into the mall. Then I almost lost her. I hurried forward. At the bottom of the escalator two businessmen blocked my way. I shoved one a little too hard.

"Hey!" he shouted. People turned and stared, including Sadie, who stood a few feet away against a wall. Beside her was a tall, thin, suit-wearing, short-haired woman. A dyke for sure and a butch to boot. I gawked, feeling the blood rise in my cheeks. Sadie's eyes locked on mine. Foolishly, I gripped the escalator handrail for support. It rolled around on its track and yanked me down. My eyes were jerked away from hers by the force, and I heard Sadie giggle. By the time I struggled back to my feet all I could see was her beautiful back as she and her butch disappeared into the lunch crowd abyss.

Now, I know some women would have taken the appearance of Sadie's girlfriend as a red light. She's taken, stay away, stop lusting after her. Me, I took it as a sign of encouragement. A challenge, not an impossibility. If she had met a man for lunch, I would have backed off. I've chased enough straight women to know what a waste of time that can be. But Sadie was clearly a femme lesbian, my favourite species, my raison d'être, the object of my tremendous desire. I smiled all the way to the office.

I was furiously pouring over flight schedules on my computer when Sadie came back from lunch. I could smell her perfume and knew she was standing right in front of my desk. I did not look up.

"You shouldn't spy on people," she said. "It's not nice. Besides, it's dangerous. You might find out something you're not supposed to know." I peered up with one eye closed, as if I was scared she would hit me. She was half smirking as she turned on her heel and swished toward her glass-enclosed, semi-private office. I guess I should have been embarrassed but I wasn't. I felt light, even happy. I had something to look forward to. Someone to chase. Work can be so boring, day after day. Some people live their whole lives and never have such a looker for a boss. Others have that kind of luck all the time. I was happy to have it just once.

Later that afternoon I felt bold. I knocked on her office door. She was standing by the filing cabinet, the top drawer open. She glanced up at me, her eyes smiling.

"Yes, Bobby? What can I do for you?"

Looking her straight in the eye I said, "If you ever need me for...anything...." I hesitated a moment to drag out my meaning, "here's my number at home." I handed her a business card, my private number scribbled on the back. Without taking her eyes off me, she reached for the card, her fingers grazing mine.

"I'll put it in a safe place," she said teasingly and I almost died when she took the card and slipped it down her shirt between her breasts. I wanted to be that card. I smiled and sparkled my eyes at her. She laughed, touched my face lightly with her hand, and went back to work.

On Friday night I went out to Rosie's, my favourite dyke bar with my best friend, Fay. We were standing near the dance floor having a beer when I saw Sadie and her girlfriend across the room, at one of the cosy, intimate tables near the wall. I watched them for a while. When the girlfriend got up to go to the women's room, Sadie walked over to where I was standing.

"What are you doing?" she whispered in my ear. I felt hot breath on my skin.

"What?" I gazed into her beautiful eyes.

"You've been watching me all night," she challenged.

I glanced down at my shoes. "Well, yes I have, but I really can't help it." I peeked up at her and she was smiling, like she was flattered, so I continued, "You really are beautiful. You're the best looking, sexiest boss I've ever worked for."

She squeezed my hand. I stared deeply into her eyes. "I just want you to know one thing," I said fearlessly. "I'm going to keep cruising you until you either say yes...or tell me to stop." She raised her eyebrows at me, amused and impressed at the same time.

Monday Sadie was later than usual. At ten o'clock the front door swung open, she hurried past my desk, marched into her office and slammed the door. All morning, she paced, she opened drawers and banged them shut, crumpled pieces of paper into tight little balls and threw them into the garbage can across the room. Then she sat at her desk, quietly staring into space. She must have had a fight with her lover. Her mood had all the markings of marital hell. I figured it was best to just stay out of her way.

At five o'clock Jerry and Jack said goodbye, but I was behind in my paperwork, so I stayed to catch up. I was deeply engrossed in my computer screen when I smelled Sadie's perfume drifting toward me. I looked up. Her deep brown eyes penetrated mine.

"Yes," she said.

"Yes?" I was in shock.

"Yes."

I shut off my screen. "Now?"

"Now."

"Here?"

She took my hand and dragged me toward the lunch area. "Here," she yanked me into the supply room and locked the door.

As much as I had been dreaming, hoping, and praying for this moment, I needed to know why. I stepped back. "What's going on?" I asked her.

She sighed deeply and leaned against stacks of *Experience Alaska* pamphlets. "The bitch has been cheating on me. All our friends know. I'm the last to find out. Why are lovers always the last to know?"

"I don't know."

"Anyway, who cares?" She held out her hand. "Come here, Bobby." I paused for a moment. She looked so beautiful in her grief, pain and passion. I wanted her more than ever. And I could see she wanted me, but for all the wrong reasons. She wanted to use me to get back at her cheating girlfriend. I could have been anybody. As for me — I'd be a homewrecker, the other woman, corrupting the morals of a married woman. I looked back at her. I didn't care. She wanted me and that's all that mattered. Ever since she walked into Gulliver's Travel, with that gorgeous body and sensuous femme charm, I knew this moment would come.

I took her outstretched hand. She pulled me to her. I raised my free hand to her beautiful, angry face and kissed her. My passion was an ancient volcano, lava building for hundreds of years inside my aching body. I poured every ounce into that first kiss. A kiss to die for, deep, wet and explosive. She pulled away and stared at me, trying to catch her breath. I waited to see what she would do. She licked her lips provocatively, then flung herself back into my arms, her mouth on mine, hard, urgent and wanting. We kissed again and I wrapped my arms around her, drawing her toward me, desperate to touch her all over. I wanted to see her naked. From the beginning I'd been watching her, undressing her with my eyes, wondering how her body would feel next to mine. I slowly began to undo the purple buttons on her silk blouse. She rested her hands lightly on my waist and watched. The smooth material slid down her arms easily. I caught the shirt as it fell and carefully hung it on the corner of a shelf. Then I stepped back a few inches to see her better. Her soft round tits spilled out over a lacy black bra.

"Feel them," she said. "I know you want to."

I raised my hands and held her breasts, enjoying the weight of them, feeling her nipples grow hard. She reached behind and undid the clasp. The elastic loosened and her bra fell into my hands. I couldn't contain myself any longer. I buried my face in her fullness. She ran her fingers through my hair and down my back.

"Take off your shirt," she ordered.

I tore at my buttons and ripped off my shirt, letting it fall to the floor near my feet. I wrapped my arms around her waist, pulling her to me tightly. My hands around her ass. She was half sitting on my thigh. I could feel her heat right through her skirt. Warm, wet and ready. I reached for her tenderly and slipped my hands under the waistband of her panties. She spread her legs. I slid my hand onto her slippery cunt. She moaned and forced herself onto my eager fingers, then I remembered. I pulled out. Big, questioning eyes looked up at me.

"What's wrong, Bobby?"

"Shit!" I said. "God I miss the seventies."

"What?"

"Safe sex. You know. We need latex gloves, a dental dam, a condom, anything."

"Oh god." Her desire for me was palpable. There had to be something we could do. I pulled free of her and looked around, then left her leaning against the shelves, out of breath and longing. I staggered into the lunchroom, searching for something, anything, that even resembled a latex glove. Desperately, I checked the fridge. My uneaten cheese sandwich from Friday sat in a clear plastic bag on the bottom rack. I laughed and lunged for it. The sandwich slipped out and I tossed it into the garbage. I went back to her, holding up my prize. She giggled as I shook out the crumbs and slid my hand into the baggie.

"Oh Bobby, don't make me wait any longer," she hissed, and I was back in her arms, my gloved hand up her dress and inside her underwear. Urgently I felt for her opening, slid one finger in. She grabbed for me with her cunt and I gave her another finger and another. The world slipped away. We were nothing but a hand and a cunt. She tore at the flesh on my back with her nails crying, "Yes, baby, yes, I want you to fuck me, don't stop." I gave her all I had to give and she took it and took it, until she was coming. Deep, heaving waves of muscles contracting on my fingers.

"Oh, Sadie. You're beautiful," I whispered in her ear, and I meant every word. I was so happy I thought I would burst.

I held her as her breathing calmed. She clutched me, body tight against mine. We were sweating onto sheets of Xerox paper. My hand still inside her. I think we were in love, just for that moment. She was still my boss. She still had a lover who cheated on her. But in that instant we were the two happiest dykes the world had ever known. I wanted it to go on forever.

I knew she would soon pull away, adjust her clothes and we'd both go home. Sadie to her lover, me to my empty apartment. We would not fall in love. She would not leave her lover for me. She would still be my boss. I would keep searching for the woman of my dreams. And yet, I knew that on Monday morning's, when I'd drag myself reluctantly into work for the start of another long week, I'd always have Sadie, the beautiful voluptuous boss-lady across the room to daydream about. I'd never forget the feel of her cunt on my hand, the softness of her breasts against mine or her powerful, womanly scent.

I reached up, stroked her hair and we stayed like that for a long time. Then I brought my lips to hers and we kissed. I felt her body moving just a little, her passion building again. I smiled because I knew the great romantics would always have Paris, Bogart and Bergman would always have Casablanca and for the rest of our lives, Sadie and I would always have Gulliver's Travel.

▼▼▼

To The Moon

▼ Jonathan Patterson orders another whisky, straight up, for the road. He has already had enough to drink, but he doesn't care. This has been the worst year of his life. The trouble started at work when his boss asked him to move ten new Laserjet printers across the store. "Sure thing," he said, then bent over, picked up a box and herniated a disc in his lower vertebrae. It left him flat on his back for six weeks and in chronic pain ever since. For nine months he's been fighting Workers' Compensation over his claim for disability benefits. The Compensation Board insists his slipped disc is a pre-existing condition, not a job-related injury, rendering Jonathan ineligible for benefits. Jonathan's lawyer remains hopeful, but he's not the one raising two kids and paying off a mortgage on his wife's salary as an accounting clerk at the bank.

The pain in Jonathan's back is only vaguely dulled by copious amounts of codeine-laced 292s, washed down with shots of Canadian Club rye whisky and beer chasers. He hasn't worked since his back went out. The final calamity occurred early that morning. Lisa, Jonathan's wife, announced she was leaving and taking their two kids with her.

Jonathan feels like a man struck down by a midnight mugger, reeling in shock. Six whiskies with chasers momentarily coat his sharp, shrill pain in a sweet, sticky oblivion.

A million thoughts whirl and stumble in Jonathan's head as he sips his drink. He sees Lisa's cold, determined face, as she tells him over breakfast she's leaving. Himself, pathetic, pleading her not to go, to give him another chance, promising things would get better soon. Her stony expression, arms folded across her chest, the phone call to her mother. The kids' teary faces and helpless little stares as she loads them in the station wagon.

"Damn her," he mutters to the bartender who has heard it all before. Jonathan can't believe this is happening to him. It wasn't supposed to be this way. He swivels on his bar stool and spots a young couple cooing at each other at a small table in a dark corner. A bitter anguish surges through his blood, leaving a bad taste in his mouth. Acid churns in the pit of his stomach. He downs the rest of his drink, disgusted with the couple's public affection. He slips down from the wooden bar stool, wavers toward the front door and staggers into the street.

A gentle wind sprays cold rain onto his face. His dark green pick-up truck is parked right outside the pub. Jonathan has a hard time getting the key into the lock. He kneels down so his eyes are inches from the keyhole and tries again. It opens. Even through the haze of alcohol, his back aches. He stands up slowly, carefully, opens the truck door and climbs into the driver's seat. Small drops of rain splatter the windshield. Jonathan searches for the wiper switch, pops the truck into first and pulls away. He turns on CFOX, the local rock station and punches the volume up to ten. Quadraphonic speakers pump loud music through Jonathan's ears. He sings along with Bruce Springsteen, *Born in the USA*. It's ten past midnight. Not much traffic on the road.

Jonathan veers on to the Georgia Viaduct and drives east.

The road curves left. He pulls the wheel sharply and almost collides with the grey cement guard-rail. The bridge arches above Vancouver's downtown east side. House lights and street lamps sparkle in the distance, pretty, like diamond sun on the ocean on a bright summer day. To the right, Jonathan notices the geodesic dome of the Omnimax Theatre, built for Expo '86, a round ball building covered with tiny glittering lights. Reminds him of a giant disco ball, of the last time he went dancing with Lisa. Her mother volunteered to babysit on a Saturday night last year, before his back screwed up. He and Lisa dressed up and went out to a popular disco in the west end. He remembered watching his wife dance. After seven years of marriage, two kids and a townhouse, Lisa was still a beautiful woman. That night, he fell in love all over again and he knew she felt it too. When the DJ played a slow song she cuddled up to him, whispered sweet things in his ear. They went home and made love.

Depression crushes grievously around Jonathan's despondent heart. His eyes brim with tears. The bridge slopes downhill and joins Prior Street, curving sharply first to the left, then to the right. Jonathan feels dizzy. Lights reflecting off the wet, black street glare in his eyes. The lights spin. The base beat of the music pounds in his brain. He leans back in his seat, one hand on his lap, the other barely touching the steering wheel. White lines dance hypnotically, like a laser show. He is suddenly exhausted. His eyes close part way. He fights to keep them open, begins to nod off. He is falling, sinking, lower and darker, the silence a welcome balm for his frayed nerves. His truck glides left. The car beside him swerves, avoiding a collision by inches, honking its horn loud. The sound jars Jonathan back to consciousness. He grips the wheel with both hands, squints to clear his blurred vision. The road is slick with rain. The truck picks up speed as he coasts down the hill toward Clark Street. The light turns red. Jonathan doesn't notice. He is not conscious of anyone else on the road.

Jonathan is vaguely aware of a dull thud against his front bumper. Through his hazy vision he sees what looks like a guy on a motorcycle jumping over his truck. He must be hallucinating. He's glad to be almost home. He shuts his eyes hard and opens them. An empty dark road. He wants nothing more than to go home, get into bed, and pull the covers over his head forever.

The ringing phone rips Leah Lapinsky from sleep. Sharp fear slices her heart. She sits bolt upright, fumbles for the receiver.

"Hello?"

"Mrs. Lapinsky? Mrs. Harvey Lapinsky?" She barely hears the words. She is hot. She pushes the covers down. Harvey looks up, grunts, rolls over and goes back to sleep. A brisk, professional voice speaks to her. The words enter her brain quietly, like a cloud passing in front of the sun, blocking the light. The voice repeats itself. Leah feels like someone has shoved her off the edge of a cliff, and she is falling down into a grand canyon, bottom so deep it can't be seen. Somewhere, through the din she hears the name of her daughter, "Toby." The voice drones on. She hears and doesn't hear. She hangs up the phone and sits in the dark room, hanging onto the quiet for a few more precious seconds. Heart beating furiously in her chest, Leah lays a hand on her husband's shoulder and shakes him awake.

They take turns in the bathroom, dress without speaking, without looking at each other. Their bodies move mechanically. Their eyes flare wide. They are both intimately familiar with tragedy and violence. Leah and Harvey met in 1946 in a displaced persons camp in Warsaw, Poland. Fifteen and sixteen respectively, each a sole survivor of their extended families.

Leah stands up from the toilet, pulls up her pants, desperately attempting to maintain her composure. Dire reality knocks brutally against her. The doctor's voice echoes inside her head. Toby. The police. An accident. Her heart lurches painfully in her chest, tearing at her resolve, threatening to conquer her. Steeling herself, one hand against the wall, Leah stops and breathes.

They speed down South Granville in Harvey's navy blue Chevy Cavalier. The rain has stopped, the wet, black road reflects neon from stores lining the street. Leah sits in a daze. Green, orange, blue signs burn in the early morning light. Tiffany's Lamps, Shaughnessey Antique Furniture, Persian Rugs, Aviv's Bakery, the old Stanley Theatre with its blue and white neon marquee and art deco design — it all seems obscenely frivolous to Leah. The extravagance of the luxury stores mocks their disaster. She looks over at Harvey and wonders how he is able to drive. His hands clutch the steering wheel. His eyes wide. He breathes quickly and loudly, in and out through his nose. Greying, uncombed hair flies in all directions on his head. Leah notices his pyjama top under his jacket.

Harvey feels Leah's stare. He won't face her. He must stay in control. He wraps an iron grip around the mush in his stomach.

"An accident. A terrible accident," the words Leah spoke when she woke him from sleep. "The hospital, at once." A jumble of crazy mixed up words, terrifying words that make your stomach heave, snap your nerves on edge.

Harvey remembers naming their baby girl. Toby, after his mother Tova, who died in the war. A happiness Harvey never thought he'd live to see bubbled around him, enveloping him in a pool of warm, luxurious delight. He cried at the first sight of his baby daughter. So tiny and perfect. A miracle. Before she was born, Harvey was a man without joy, without faith in the future. But his daughter was born in Canada in 1967, twenty-two years after his living hell, a walking skeleton at Bergen Belsen. It was a miracle. At the age of thirty-seven, Leah gave birth to a healthy baby girl. They had tried for years to have children. The doctor said Leah's miscarriages were a result of her years at Treblinka. Eleven years old when she was taken, didn't start menstruating until eighteen, her body never fully recovered from the trauma. The doctor said she couldn't have children. It was a miracle. Harvey's world burst into sunshine when in middle age, against all hope, he had a beautiful, healthy and free baby girl. Little Toby Lapinsky, her brown eyes deep, dark, serious and sorrowful, as if she'd already glimpsed the worst of the world, as if she'd already lived her life before it even began.

"An accident. A terrible accident." Twisted, tangled, unthinkable words, under the stark, terrifying, knife-edged truth. "Toby. An accident." His daughter's name rising from the aftermath.

Leah stares out the window as they race to St. Paul's hospital in the west end. Over the Granville Bridge she sees tall stacks of high-rise apartment buildings and the lights over False Creek. The glittering dome reminds Leah of a big shiny golf ball. On the other side of the bridge they pass several cheap motels, The Cecil, The Austin. Drunk men gather outside, talking loudly. Fighting, laughing, lingering.

Harvey turns onto Davie Street. At one in the morning the area is alive with people milling about on the sidewalks, eating slices of pizza, laughing, holding hands, walking home from the bars. The street is especially crowded in front of a large night-club called Jupiter, where people spill out from the darkened bar. Harvey stops at a red light in front of the bar and Leah turns to stare. Most of the people are scantily dressed men. Some are in groups, some stand alone, some appear inebriated. Leah spots a few unusually tall women, dressed lavishly in high heels and evening dresses. She sees a young man in tight leather pants, white shirt and leather jacket lean against the brick wall. Another man, similarly dressed in ripped blue jeans approaches the first. A jagged pain scrapes across Leah's heart. Both are wearing the kind of jacket Toby usually wears.

Leah wraps her arms around herself. Pictures of Toby float freely in her head. Toby's angry face during their last visit. Another fight. Toby furious. Always mad at her. Flew out of the apartment, just like she'd done ten years before, a storm leaving home. Slamming the door behind. Shaking the foundation of their lives.

An accident. A terrible accident. Come right away. Leah flattens her foot on an imaginary gas peddle, wills Harvey to drive faster. Wishes she could fly. Fly to her daughter. Her only daughter. Her only child. A chill shoots through her. Out the window, in the sky, she sees movement, the motion of flying. She sees wings flutter like the shadow of a bird. Street lights play tricks. The shadow darts toward her, closer, closer. She looks into its eyes. Her eyes. Soft, angry, sorrowful, deep brown eyes pierce Leah's heart. Toby.

Every hair on Leah's body stands on end. The shadow swoops up and away, into the dark night sky. Ominous sky, a great hole of nothingness soars all the way to the heavens, the stars. All the way to the moon. Leah feels a punch in her stomach. And she is running, floating, flying after her daughter, her baby. Leah remembers changing her diapers,

Toby laughing and rubbing her tiny feet together. A million years ago. An accident. A terrible accident.

"Mrs. Lapinsky? Mrs. Harvey Lapinsky? Come right away..."

Leah remembers the day Toby sat nervously across from her at the kitchen table. "I'm gay," she said. "I'm a lesbian. You remember Marsha? From school? Well, she's more than just a friend."

More than a friend. Toby. An accident. Why doesn't the car drive faster? Harvey, faster. My Toby. My baby. Seems like just yesterday. The first time Toby walked on her own, Leah was on the phone with her friend Miriam. Toby was across the room. Leah only half paying attention. The baby pulled herself up by the kitchen chair like she'd been doing it all her life. She let go and put one foot in front of the other, across the kitchen's tile floor in the old one-bedroom apartment with leaky pipes and thin walls. Toby's diaper sagging in back, as always, such a tiny baby. Her little arms straight out in front. Her legs wobbly. Face set in deep concentration and focused determination. A small drop of saliva dribbled from the corner of her mouth. She walked toward her mother. Leah watched her daughter. My baby. Walking. "Come to Mama." Toby gazed up at her mother and smiled. The grin on her face brilliant, a late afternoon sun breaking through a cloudy day. Leah laughed out loud. "That's it baby. Come to Mama." An accident. A terrible accident. Come right away. Faster Harvey. Faster. My baby.

An hour earlier, Toby Lapinsky got up from the couch and kissed her lover Chris. Tomorrow was their six-month anniversary. They couldn't be happier. Toby was in love. She was going home to her own apartment. Her cat Felix hadn't had dinner and she didn't have the heart to make him wait until morning. Chris tried to convince her to spend the night, wound her arms around Toby's neck, gently pushed her up against the fridge door, slipped a bare thigh between her lover's legs. She kissed Toby, sweet and sensuous, all over her face, tongue darting in her ear.

"Come on baby..." she begged, "let's go back to bed."

Toby laughed, held Chris tightly around the waist and kissed her sweet beautiful lover. Chris slid her whole body up and down against Toby, knocking fridge magnets to the floor. Toby was lost in her lover's embrace, lost in spicy, magic hands touching her all over. Gentle, passionate caresses. Toby moaned softly, not wanting to leave, ever. She gathered every ounce of discipline and pulled away.

"Gotta go babe. Really I do. I'll see you tomorrow night after work. I've got a great idea."

Toby waved goodbye. Chris remained in the bedroom window watching the back parking lot. Toby slipped her key in the ignition and started up her bike. It hadn't been running well lately, so she warmed it up longer than usual. The neighbours might complain. It was past midnight, but she took the chance anyway. A light rain started to fall. She closed the zipper on her black leather jacket and smiled to herself as she mounted her bike and fastened her helmet. Tomorrow was Friday night, she was taking Chris to a new gay restaurant on Robson Street. She already knew they had Chris's favourite dish, three cheese lasagna, on the menu.

Toby jerked the bike off its kickstand and backed out of the parking lot, pushing off with her feet. Glancing once more up to Chris's window she smiled, drove into the street and up the hill. Not many cars on the road, just the way Toby liked it.

Chris dropped her bathrobe to the floor and slipped into bed. She secured the covers snugly and hugged herself, pretending Toby was still with her, then she drifted to sleep. Moments later she sat up suddenly. Woken by a crash in her dream. Her heart pounded in her chest. She scanned the dark room and tried to place the source of her fear. When she couldn't, she calmed herself by thinking pleasant thoughts. She remembered the first time she met Toby, at a women's dance. Chris had gone with her best friend Julie and Julie's new lover, Angela. Julie and Angela had been dancing since the three had arrived. Chris stood alone against a wall glancing around, watching, sipping a glass of red wine. Toby leaned against the opposite wall, drinking a cold beer from the bottle, girl-watching from her favourite spot by the corner speakers. She'd been checking out Chris for some time. Chris felt her gaze from across the room, turned and saw a short, athletic butch in a black leather jacket and tight blue jeans. They stayed where they were for a long time, watching, waiting. Finally, Toby made the first move. She crossed the room, strobe lights flashing in her face, accentuating her strong, handsome features. Smiling, she stopped in front of Chris. Her deep brown soulful eyes radiated a sad, resplendent light which penetrated Chris to her core. Without a word, Toby held out her hand. Chris took it and let the small, mysterious woman lead her to the dance floor. Their meeting always reminded Chris of Tony and Maria in *West Side Story*, where the two lovers-to-be move slowly toward each other across a crowded dance floor. The camera fades everyone else out of focus as the starry-eyed Tony and Maria meet in the middle of the room. Chris loved romance. She believed in fate with all her heart. She knew Toby and her were meant to be. The memory soothed her and she drifted back to sleep.

Toby shifted her bike into third gear. Tires gripped damp pavement. It had been a long week and she was tired. She wondered whether there was milk in the fridge for her morning coffee, almost stopped at the 24-hour store to buy some, then decided to go straight home. She didn't mind her coffee black. She rode through the intersection at the corner of Clark and Venables. She didn't see the dark green truck accelerating toward her through a red light. Her peripheral vision was reduced with her full face helmet, just enough to hide the truck's reckless, wavering approach. It felt like a dream when the metal hit her, hurtling her leather-clad body through the air. The bike slipped out from between her legs, scraped across the pavement and crashed against a car parked by the side of the road. Toby was above it all, watching her body catapult twenty feet in the air and fly, like a night bird in slow motion, all the way to the stars, all the way to the moon. Then she fell, fast, faster, landing hard on the wet greasy pavement. The crack was either the helmet or her head. Then she didn't hear anything at all. Not the truck's tires screeching down the street. Not the shrill slam of brakes as the car behind swerved to avoid her crumpled body. Not the wailing ambulance or the police or the murmur of the small crowd that gathered, one by one, in morbid curiosity.

Toby did not hear a thing.

Jonathan Patterson veered his truck sharply to the right when he recognized his street. His house was at the top of the hill, his vehicle slowed naturally. He was fighting to stay awake as he lurched to the right of the road, bumped over the curb and onto the lawn, where the truck rolled to a stop. He switched the ignition off, lowered his head onto the steering wheel and he fell into a deep and troubled sleep.

When there is nothing more to be done, Leah and Harvey shuffle wordlessly down the hospital corridor. In a small smoking lounge a young, emaciated man in green pyjamas slumps in a wheelchair, a cigarette burning between fingers hanging down the side of his chair in total defeat. A second young man, in street clothes, kneels on the floor in front of him, quietly weeping, his head in his friend's lap. Harvey holds his breath, so as not to cry out. Leah moves alongside her husband, in shock. Every inch of skin on her body vibrates. Her senses are acute. Her nerves burn. Her heart beats a million miles an hour in her inner ear. Other sounds echo, muted and dull. A mother's wail longs to rise to the surface and be free. Leah stares straight ahead, concentrating on the clip, clip of her shoes along the polished hospital floor. Fearful she will fall over the edge, that the weight of her grief will drag her down into bottomless despair. She is vaguely aware of Harvey, plodding along beside her. He reaches over, gently grasps her hand. Nurses, orderlies and cleaning staff give the distraught couple wide berth as they manoeuvre through the quiet, late-night halls.

The drive home is time in a padded cell. Silently they travel through the sleeping city to the third floor of a four story walk-up. Harvey opens the front door of their apartment. Leah mechanically follows him back to their bedroom. Hours earlier, their room had been a safe haven from the cold world, where they slept, watched TV, read the paper, shared a bed. Now it's the scene of the accident, the place where they first heard the terrible news. Leah feels faint with dread. She sits on the edge of the bed and her body begins to shake, quietly. A whole world of sorrow pushes up in Leah. Her belly rises to her throat. She throws back her head and wails. Harvey sits beside her, silent. Waves of grief flow from Leah, loosening the iron grip around his heart. He cries out, his voice soaring up to the sky, to the stars, all the way to the moon.

Somewhere, submerged under many layers in the back of Leah's mind, she knows she will have to call Toby's friends and tell them the news. Toby had a new girlfriend. What was her name? Carrie? Cathy?

Chris doesn't know why Toby doesn't phone her or arrive for their date on Friday night. There's no answer at her place. She didn't show up for work. No one knows where she is. Not even Sal.

When she has exhausted all other options, Chris dials the number to Toby's parents.

▼▼▼

The Gay Divorcée

▼ Five months ago, my whole life changed.

One week before our sixth anniversary, Jacquie dumped me for Spike Goldstein, a softball player and accountant who lives in our apartment building, two floors down. I almost fell over in shock. We were sitting at the kitchen table eating supper, and as the reality of what Jacquie said settled in, my fajita-filled fork clattered onto my plate and my heart exploded in my chest. Her words were a blur, as if I was listening to someone speak a foreign language. I heard fragments of sentences, isolated words and half thoughts.

"Can't go on like this...over...still be friends...haven't been happy...you know as well as I do...we've been moving apart...sorry...hurts me too...." She cried while she spoke.

I sat in my seat, mouth gaping and stared. My pulse raced adrenalin through my veins. Her decision splintered my heart into a million tiny pieces, ripped a hole in my chest clear through to the other side. Strangely, I was also calm. Loss was nothing new to me. It had been five years since my friend Alex died of AIDS. My grandfather passed away shortly after and I lost my friend Judy last September. The knowledge that Jacquie was not dying, only leaving, was the one thought that held me together. I sat, listened and did not speak. What was there to say?

For months I wallowed in despair, shock, pain, and

humiliation. Jacquie and I had been known in the community as one of the few long-term couples who were "making it." Although we hadn't wanted to be, we were role models for other women. During the first three months of our break-up I was so raw and exposed I could barely leave the house. Every cell in my body vibrated with pain. I'd go to sleep sad and wake up horrified. My pride, self esteem and ego plummeted, splattering twenty stories onto a grease-covered back alley, alone and badly bruised. While Jacquie and Spike lived happily ever after, I drank too much scotch, showed up late for work, watched "I Love Lucy" reruns, cried on friends' shoulders, smoked grass, felt sorry for myself, made rude comments in public about my ex and her current, cried, carried on and generally became known throughout town as a bitter homosexual.

Bitter or not, I have never been the celibate type. I knew I could be in misery and grief and be fucking my brains out at the same time. And I was out to prove it. There was no doubt about my pain. It was visible on my face, exuding from my body, echoing through my broken heart and thrashing around inside my empty belly. In the end, only time and deep therapy would truly heal me. I needed to rebuild my broken pride from within, nurse my wounds, reaffirm my reason to live, find strength in my own heart and learn to love myself. In the loneliest, bleakest hours of our lives, our selves are all we can really count on. But, for the moment, my thinking was far more shallow. I needed to be appreciated. I wanted to be chased, to be loved, held, stroked, licked, kissed, touched and taken. My body cried out for caresses, and even in my sorrow, I was horny as hell. After five months of suffering, I was moving to a new emotional place.

"If you know anyone who's ever had a crush on me," I

told my friends, "Give her my phone number and tell her it's a good time to call."

My mission had begun. Or so I thought. After six years of marriage to Jacquie, I was out of practise. A lot of things had changed. Women were younger. There was safe sex to worry about. I had aged. Would women still find me attractive? I wasn't sure where to start. I was beside myself with panic. I ran to the phone and called Bobby Silverstein, my cousin and big time babe-ifyer about town.

"Okay," she said. "We'll start with the obvious. Who do you have the hots for?"

I thought about it and drew a blank. "I don't know."

"What?"

"I haven't been looking Bobby, you know that."

"Kayla. You can't think of anybody? Someone you know from the gym? The bar? How about work?"

No one came to mind.

"Come on. There must be somebody."

"I told you. I haven't been looking."

"Well looking is the first thing you need to do. Are you sure there isn't somebody?"

"Of course I'm sure. I was happily married."

"Kayla, it's me you're talking to. I know you've looked around. You've told me yourself. Wasn't there some woman you were lusting after just last year?"

"No! I already told you I can't think of anyone, okay?"

"Oh boy."

"What?"

"This might be harder than I thought."

"Don't say that," I groaned. "You're depressing me."

"Okay. Sorry. Look, I'll be right over. We can't do this over the phone. You're in bad shape."

"Oh thanks."

"Go take a shower or something to clear your head. I'll be there in half an hour."

She brought over a six pack of beer, warm, but we opened two anyway, and a copy of *Flaunt It*, our local queer paper. Bobby opened the classified ads on my coffee table. Bright red ink already circled a few ads. Bobby dialled the classified number and thrust the receiver into my hand. A computer voice explained the rules.

"Welcome to Queer Connections classifieds. A charge of ninety-six cents a minute will automatically be billed to your home number. At the tone, punch in the box number of the ad that interests you."

I chose one of the circled ads. A woman's voice repeated the print ad word for word, then asked me to leave a message after the tone. I eyed Bobby for help. She shrugged.

"Uh..." I began eloquently, "I saw your ad." Oh brilliant. "And uh, I live in Vancouver and I'm recently single and..." I referred to the ad, "I see that you like to go dancing. So, uh, let's meet. Okay? I...look forward to meeting, uh, hearing from you. Okay. Bye." I banged down the receiver.

Bobby shook her head. "You forgot to leave your phone number."

"Oh shit. You think I should call her back?"

"I don't know. She'll either think it's endearing or she'll think you're a nerd. Hard to say."

"Great. I'm not calling back. This is nerve-wracking."

"Uh huh." Bobby dialled the number again and handed me the receiver.

"Again?"

"Pick a different box number."

I tried another one. A soft, sexy voice said she was a well-endowed femme looking for butches to satisfy her. No walks on the beach, movies or dinners, she just wanted sex. I left my name, number and tried to sound sexy and charming. I hung up the phone and beamed.

Bobby picked it back up. "Do more. They won't all call back."

"Really?"

"Uh huh."

I called all the ads Bobby had circled.

"Now what?"

"Well, it'll take a few days before you get any responses, so now we go to the bar."

"What? Bobby, I've barely even looked at another woman in six years. Don't you think this is enough for one night?"

"Hell no. Come on. You've been miserable and depressed for six months."

"Five," I broke in defensively.

"Okay five. Enough is enough. It's time to get out there. Go get changed. We're going out."

I sighed and trundled, somewhat reluctantly, into the bedroom.

At the club I bought us each a beer. We stood near the dance floor, watching. The bar was in a basement with low ceilings and black walls. The carpet was red. Purple blacklights lit up every piece of fluff on dark shirts, white t-shirts glowed fluorescent and everyone's teeth looked green. In the centre of the dance floor, a medium-sized disco ball bounced beams of white light circling and spinning around the room.

Bobby was telling a tasteless joke about blonde travel agents when I saw Ana. I couldn't remember her name at first, but I remembered her. Long black curly hair, deep dark eyes, full mouth, cheekbones for days, and a curvy voluptuous body encased in tight black spandex shorts under a short purple skirt. On top she wore nothing but a black sports bra. She had the widest smile and the warmest eyes. I was instantly enchanted from across the room, as I had been once before. We had met over a year ago. We talked. I bought her a drink. We danced. We laughed. I walked her to her car, we kissed. Melted into each other, without a word, riding with the night air, the wind. Until I remembered I was married. Remembered who I was and the choices I had made. I broke from her grasp suddenly. Without explanation, I ran and didn't look back.

Now here she was again, on the other side of the bar, dancing with someone I'd never seen before. I watched, trying to determine if they were friends or lovers. They danced a few feet apart, occasionally leaning toward each other to talk and laugh. They looked around more than they looked at each other. Definitely friends. No sexual heat between them. I turned to Bobby. She was staring at me.

"Who are you looking at?" She strained above the music.

I nodded my head toward the dance floor. "That's Ana."

"Who?"

"Remember? I met her last year. She used to live here. She's from Mexico City. She was up here studying at UBC, a political science major. I almost went home with her one night, that time when Jacquie was back east visiting her family. Remember?"

Bobby pointed her finger at me. "I told you! I knew there was someone."

I shrugged sheepishly. "Nothing happened. I walked her to her car and we kissed. Then I chickened out and bolted." I shook my head. "She probably thought I was a total nerd. Last I heard she was living in California. Haven't seen her since."

Bobby looked over at Ana, checking her out. "So that's her? Looks good."

"Good? Are you crazy? She's beautiful."

"So? If that's how you feel, go ask her to dance."

"You think I should?"

Bobby shook her head and frowned.

"Okay. I'm going."

As I crossed the dance floor to Ana, I recalled the night when I'd kissed her. I walked her to her car and we stood and talked. I spoke to her in Spanish. I didn't know much, but I did know how to say, *Que bonitos ojos tienes*, what beautiful eyes you have. She smiled back and moved closer. It was one of those perfect moments. The night was warm. Music drifted across the street from the club. Her perfume lured me closer. Her brown eyes drew me in. My lips were on hers, my arms around her waist. Her soft body pressed against me. I was floating on a wave of desire, cheating on my girlfriend and I couldn't stop myself. Her mouth felt too good, her kisses too sweet, her touch too tantalizing, our passion too potent. We wrapped our arms around each other, crazy with hunger. She asked me to come home with her. I wanted to, but the consequences of crossing that line were more than I was prepared to deal with. I ran. It was the last I saw her.

Across the dance floor, I stopped a few feet from Ana. She looked at me blankly, then her face lit up. "Hola," she said, her beautiful brown eyes smiling.

"*Como estas?*' I grinned back.

"*Bien, gracias.* I'm back in Vancouver."

"I can see that."

"*Momentito.*" She held up a finger and leaned over, whispering something to her friend. Her friend looked over at me and shrugged, then walked off the dance floor.

"Dance?" Ana asked.

"My pleasure."

I started to move my hips and arms to the music, careful to keep a few feet back, to give her space. She moved right up against me, pushing her pelvis seductively in my direction. My heart fluttered and I felt my whole body respond. I swallowed hard and smiled at her.

She came in real close and whispered in my ear, "So? How are things with you?"

"Okay, but me and Jacquie broke up."

She backed away and looked me in the eye. "Oh." She shook her head, then moved back in, closer. "How are you doing?"

"Okay. It's been hard. I'm much better now." I slipped an arm around her waist. She rested a hand on my shoulder and we danced through the rest of the song. She had a sexy femme way of dancing, moving her hips in a circular motion, lightly touching my thighs with all parts of her body. With her free hand, she held the edge of her skirt and swung it around. Tight spandex shorts covered her skin like black paint. She kept her face close to mine. I could almost feel her lips on my skin. I wanted to kiss her.

"You know, I think about you sometimes," she whispered.

"You do?"

"Uh huh." She grazed her lips against my neck. "I wonder what might have happened between us, if we'd continued that night." Her tongue darted inside my ear. Oh my god. This was too good to be true. My first night out as a single babe and I had a beautiful woman wrapped in my arms, talking sweet, looking sexy. A miracle. She was flirting with me. No, more than that. She was cruising me. My stomach turned over.

She pulled back again and gazed at me. I stared into her serious eyes. Her lips were calling out. There was only one thing to do, I leaned forward and kissed her, lightly. She threw her arms around my neck and kissed me hard. I squeezed her to me, kissing her, long and deep, tongue around tongue. The taste of her inside me, rushing down to my liquid belly, circling, rising with the rhythm of her breath. My senses heightened, intensified with memories of the time we kissed before. I opened my eyes to look at her. She was beautiful. I kissed her face. She moaned. I moved down to her neck, tasted the salt of her sweat. She was pressing her cunt against my leg. My blood pulsated, pounded in my belly, stirring delicious pleasure, rising in sweet, searing waves.

"Hey. Why don't you two get a room?" a voice asked. We stopped kissing and glanced over. A woman dancing beside us smirked.

"Isn't this a room?" I shot back, pleased with myself. Ana laughed, then gave me a solemn, sexy look. She grasped my hand, squeezed and lay it on her waist. "Maybe she's right," she said.

"Mmmm," I agreed, smiling at her.

"How about my place?"

"Are you inviting me?"

"You know I am."

"Hang on a second." I went over to tell Bobby I was leaving.

"You rogue," she winked at me. "I want all the details tomorrow."

"Thanks for dragging me out."

I raced back to Ana.

She opened her car doors and we slipped in, Ana behind the wheel. She turned to me. I slid sideways, closer to her.

She snatched up a hard cover textbook that lay between us on the seat and tossed it into the back. She grabbed the collar of my jacket, pulling me in. We kissed in a fury. Intense, urgent and passionate. We moaned. I reached up and caressed one of her breasts with my hand.

"Oh god," she said. "Come on. Let's go to my place."

"Okay." Still leaning over her, I kissed her neck and squeezed her nipple between my fingers.

"Okay." She pressed against my hand, making no move to start the car.

"Good idea." I leaned into her lips and we kissed again.

"Okay," she repeated, breathless.

"Okay," I whispered back, running my tongue along her neckline.

"Oohh." Her hands strayed to the back of my neck, into my hair.

"You smell great." My tongue explored the space between her breasts.

"You feel amazing," she reclined further back against the door.

We couldn't get enough. We were left brain lesbians, focused on nothing but our bodies, hurtling through white water rapids, spinning and swirling down a rushing river. Unrestrained.

"Okay." She tore herself away, pushed me back to the passenger seat. I was breathing hard. We both were. I bent to kiss her again.

"Stop," she laughed. "We'll never get home this way."

Ana started the car and pulled into traffic. I clasped her free hand and held it as she drove, squeezing and stroking, grabbing and holding. I brought her hand to my lips, sucking, biting her middle finger. She turned to me, eyes smouldering. I rubbed her palm over my face. She broke free, ran her fingers through my curly black hair.

"Where do you live?" I asked breathless.

"Not far," she panted. "Just off Commercial."

"Me too."

I brought her roaming hand down to my lap, left it on my thigh as my fingers travelled slowly up her bare arm. Goose bumps formed on her skin. I caressed her harder, up to her shoulder and back down again. I leaned closer and kissed her neck. The car made a sharp right turn and stopped. She shifted into park and reached for me, hands on both sides of my face. We kissed furiously, grunting and moaning, tongues and teeth exploring and sucking. I didn't know if we were in her driveway or somebody else's. I didn't care. I pushed her back against the car door. The plastic panel between the bucket seats dug painfully into my side as I struggled to get closer to her. She grabbed my t-shirt, trying to get it over my head. She gave up on my shirt and plunged her hands underneath it, groping for my tits. I kissed up and down her neck. My legs were squeezed tight, my hot clit throbbed. Her skirt was hiked up and she opened her legs wider. I thrust my pelvis into her crotch. I tugged at the waistband of her shorts.

"*Querida*." She kissed my lips, her tongue a torrential downpour of lust. I tumbled alongside her, carried on a flood of fervent desire. "Let's go inside." Her hands gripped my shoulders. "It's too small in here."

Inside, she led me to her bedroom. The blinds were open, moonlight fell across the bed. I waited in the middle of the room as she lit a candle and placed a CD into a portable player on her dresser. She sauntered toward me, threw her arms around my neck. I held her waist. She started to dance with me.

"Pretend we are still in the bar," she whispered in my ear. "On the dance floor, like before." She pressed her body against mine, raised her face and we kissed. We were breathing faster. I reached over and removed her bra. Her nipples were erect.

"Squeeze them," she said. "I like it hard. Yeah. That's good."

She tore at my t-shirt, peeled it off and tossed it on the floor.

"We are still in the bar," she said, rubbing against my naked chest, "and I want you to fuck me." She seized three fingers on my right hand and squeezed them. I moaned. I eased her shorts and skirt down to her ankles. She stepped out of them and slid her naked body up and down my legs. I groped in my back pocket for a small leather case, which I opened. I removed a latex glove and grazed it all over her skin. I dropped to my knees and licked her leg, from the ankle up. I stood, rubbing my shoulder against her clit as I rose.

"I want you inside me," she insisted.

I snapped the glove onto my hand, kissing her furiously. Even through the glove I could feel how wet she was. Slippery. Warm. Her need engulfed the tips of my fingers. I slid one in.

"Oh god," she said. "We are still in the bar. Everyone is watching. You are fucking me in the bar."

Her fantasy burned through me. There was something torridly sexy about taking her on the dance floor in front of other hot babes. "Oh yeah, you're so wet. So open. Ready for me."

"Yeah baby. More. Put more in."

I did as she asked.

"Oh yeah," she said, "Just like that, slow. Uh huh. Oh yeah Kayla, fuck me."

"I am."

"Please."

"Yeah baby."

"Don't stop."

"Never."

"Use your thumb on my clit," she ordered and gripped my hand to show me, as her tongue plunged inside my ear. "Slow circles. Okay?"

"Anything." My fingers inside her, rotating slightly, my thumb worked circles around her hard, wet clit.

"Oh baby." She was rocking on my fingers. "And now the bartender is walking over this way."

"Yeah?" I kept moving in circles, just how she liked it.

"She's mad at us."

"Uh huh?"

"She's going to kick us out. She's telling us to leave."

She moved faster on my thumb. Her breathing sped up. "But we can't stop. Oh don't stop!" she screamed. "Please. Oh please. Yeah. Oh, I'm going to come."

I was going to come too, just from listening to her. I kept rolling my thumb. I could feel her clit throb. I could feel her heart and pulse speed up. Her teeth clamped down on my neck. Pain and pleasure coursed through my blood.

"Yeah Kayla. Oohh, baby that's good. Ohhh, yeah!" She flung her whole body tight against me, lunged deeper onto my fingers. I sensed her soul break free as her body convulsed on my hand. Her voice burst through the night air, loud, impetuous. Every part of her pulsed and quivered, aftershocks relentlessly trembled, as she came.

After a while her body relaxed. She slumped against my chest. I held her tightly around the waist and eased her over to the bed. We lay down and I held her in my arms. Her breathing calmed. Then it was kind of weird, because while laying in Ana's arms, I thought about Jacquie. In my sadness, I hugged Ana tighter. Her body felt nice, warm and soft, but laying with her like that, I thought about my ex, my old life and everything I had lost. My eyes filled with tears, which slowly rolled down my cheeks. Ana opened her eyes and wiped my face with her hand.

"It's okay," she murmured. But it wasn't. Nothing had been okay for a long time. It was a turning point in my life, terrifying and lonely. I was on a journey, part way across a rickety, wooden, suspension bridge, high above a deep, mountain canyon. No railings or hand-guard, no safety net at all. And only room enough for one to pass. Far in the distance, engulfed in a haze, the other side was barely visible. It had no form, no shape. I couldn't see much of anything and I knew I wouldn't be able to for a long, long time. The unknowable future was frightening as was each step toward it.

Six months ago I'd have told you Jacquie and I would be together forever. Who knows? Maybe we were. Maybe forever was just a little shorter than we originally thought.

Yiddish/Hebrew Glossary

bubbe: grandmother

drek: garbage; inferior merchandise or work

Err hot aygen far dir: he has eyes for you

farshteis: do you understand?

faygela: literally — little bird; homosexual, usually male

kosher: religious dietary laws, which include forbidding eating pig meat and eating meat and dairy together.

kvetchy: whiny, a complainer

latkes: pancakes

mamelah: term of endearment

matzah meal: ground matzah, like bread crumbs

minyan: quorum of ten men necessary for public worship — in progressive or reform synagogues women can be included

mishegus: craziness

oy vey: expression of surprise, as in oh my god, woe is me

shiva: seven days of mourning after a death, usually held in immediate relatives home. Every day people drop by to pay respects

shlepping:	dragging
shmata:	literally a rag, also a kerchief
sholom aleichem:	peace unto you
shul:	synagogue
tallis:	prayer shawl
yarmulke:	prayer cap
zayde:	grandfather

Photo: Susan Stewart

Karen X. Tulchinsky is a Jewish lesbian writer who lives in Vancouver. Her work has appeared in numerous anthologies including *Sister and Brother, Afterglow, Getting Wet* and *The Femme Mystique*. She has written news and reviews for *Deneuve, 10 Per Cent, Dykespeak, Xtra West, Angles* and *Fuse* magazines. She is co-editor of *Tangled Sheets: Stories and Poems of Lesbian Lust* (Women's Press, 1995) and of *Queer View Mirror : Lesbian and Gay Short, Short Fiction*. She is currently working on a novel, a play and several new anthologies.